PUFFIN BOOKS

IN BLACK AND WHIT

Martin dresses u[...]
old house as a jo[...] [...]y
fascinated with it. O[...] [...]g en-
counter on the stairs [...] [...]ether his
imagination is running [...]

In this collection of stra[...] creepy stories, only
Jenny knows that she could [...]ave managed to appear
twice in the school photo; Gary becomes strangely
moody when he takes the old miser's two-shilling coin in
change; Jean's compost heap seems to take on a life of its
own; and a mysterious correspondent breaks Dennis's
secret code.

Frightening, poignant and sometimes humorous, these
stories all display the skill which singles out Jan Mark as
perhaps the most gifted writer of short stories for today's
young. Among many awards, Jan Mark has won the
Carnegie Medal twice, for *Thunder and Lightnings* and
Handles, and this immensely entertaining collection,
bringing together as it does a number of old favourites
with four new stories, can only enhance a formidable
reputation.

Jan Mark grew up in Kent and attended the Canterbury
College of Art. She went on to teach art at Gravesend.
She started her writing career in 1973 and since then has
written a large number of highly successful books, for
which she has been awarded the Carnegie Medal and
other prestigious prizes. She spent two years as writer-in-
residence at Oxford Polytechnic and now lives in Oxford.

JAN MARK

In Black and White

Illustrated by Neil Reed

PUFFIN BOOKS

PUFFIN BOOKS

Published by the Penguin Group
Penguin Books Ltd, 27 Wrights Lane, London w8 5TZ, England
Penguin Books USA Inc., 375 Hudson Street, New York, New York 10014, USA
Penguin Books Australia Ltd, Ringwood, Victoria, Australia
Penguin Books Canada Ltd, 10 Alcorn Avenue, Toronto, Ontario, Canada M4V 3B2
Penguin Books (NZ) Ltd, 182–190 Wairau Road, Auckland 10, New Zealand

Penguin Books Ltd, Registered Offices: Harmondsworth, Middlesex, England

This collection first published by Viking 1991
Published in Puffin Books 1992
10 9 8 7 6 5 4 3 2 1

The following stories have been previously published:
'Nule' first published in *Nothing To Be Afraid Of* (Viking Kestrel) 1980;
'They Wait' first published in *They Wait* (Pepper Press) 1983; 'Who's
a Pretty Boy, Then?' first published in *Black Eyes* (Pepper Press) 1981;
'Welcome, Yule' first published in *An Oxford Book of Christmas Stories*
(Hamish Hamilton) 1986; 'Efflorescence' first published in *Beware,
Beware* (Oxford University Press) 1986.

Filmset in Linotron Baskerville

Printed in England by Clays Ltd, St Ives plc

Contents

For Martyn and Cherrill

In Black and White

Jenny Fielding is Mrs Sanderson, now. She has a husband, two daughters, Julia and Margery, and three grandchildren. On the sideboard in the living room stand photographs of them all; daughters, sons-in-law, granddaughters, grandson. Every year Julia and Margery send new school photographs of Angus, Alice and Rose. Mrs Sanderson arranges them on the sideboard and puts last year's photographs in her dressing-table drawer.

On the wall, above the sideboard, hangs Mr Sanderson's school photograph. It is black and white and a metre long, the whole school in it together. One after another Angus and Alice and Rose have asked, 'Grandpa, how was it done?' and Mr Sanderson explains that once upon a time all school photographs were like that, and had to be taken with a special camera. Everybody was arranged in a huge semicircle – there were seven hundred people at his school, and the camera, which was clockwork, slowly turned, panning from one end of the curve to the other. The real miracle is that, in the photograph, everyone is standing in a straight line while the building behind them looks curved. Grandpa tries to show them why, but they can never quite understand.

'You had to stand absolutely still,' Mr Sanderson says, 'because you could never be sure when the camera was pointing exactly at you.'

Angus and Alice and Rose love it when he gets to that point because they know what is coming next. Mr Sanderson is in the middle of the fourth row, looking very young and serious, with a surprising amount of hair, but at either end of the second row are the Schofeldt Triplets.

'Really, they were twins, Marcus and Ben,' Mr Sanderson tells them, 'and they were standing one each end of the row. When the camera got half-way round Ben left his place and ran along the back of the others, faster than the camera was moving, and went to stand beside Marcus at the other end. They got into a terrible row when they were found out, but we all thought they were heroes because we'd been forbidden to do it.'

Then Angus, Alice and Rose look closely at Grandpa's school photograph to admire the three identical and heroic Schofeldt Twins, Ben at one end, Ben and Marcus at the other.

'Lots of school photographs had mysterious identical twins at each end,' Grandpa boasts, 'but I bet ours was the only one with triplets.'

'Did you have a school photograph, Granny?' Rose asks.

'I did once,' Mrs Sanderson says, vaguely, 'but I must have lost it.'

She hates lying, but if she told the truth about her school photograph no one would believe her anyway, so she pretends it is lost. But at the back of her dressing-table drawer, where Angus and Alice and Rose also lie, growing older and larger each year, is Jenny Fielding's school photograph, still rolled into a cylinder as it was on the day she first brought it home, forty years ago. She has never shown it to anyone since.

Jenny was thirteen, in the third year, when the notice was given out in assembly that the photographer was coming the following Monday. Miss Shaw, the form teacher, had a few words of her own to add when they returned to the classroom.

'You will all make sure that your uniforms are clean and pressed, that your hair is tidy – you'd better plait yours, Maureen Blake – and your shoes polished. I do not *care* if nobody can see your feet. There will be a rehearsal on Friday, so that each girl knows where she is to stand. And wherever you stand on Friday,' said Miss Shaw, fixing them with an iron gaze, 'you will stand on Monday. On these occasions there are always certain stupid people who imagine that it is amusing to run from one end of the line to the other in order to appear twice. Anyone who does that will be dealt with severely. Do I make myself clear?'

3a gazed back at her unblinkingly. Miss Shaw, as always, had made herself very clear. But in the back row Jenny's great friend Margery Fletcher turned her head slightly and muttered to Jenny, 'I bet it will be one of us. I have a feeling.'

'Did you speak, Margery?' Miss Shaw inquired, knowing perfectly well.

'I just said I thought I might get my hair cut,' Margery said, pleasantly. 'For the photograph, you know.'

'An excellent idea,' Miss Shaw said. Margery's hair, like Jenny's, was wild and dark and curly. They were very alike in other ways, too; exactly the same height, short and stocky, and were often mistaken for each other by people who saw them misbehaving from a distance. Margery misbehaved far more frequently, and far more inventively, than Jenny, but when Jenny was falsely accused Margery always raised her hand and owned up. And on the rarer occasions when the mistake was in Jenny's favour, Jenny did the same. That was why they were best friends, faithful and true. They went everywhere together, near enough.

It had come as a surprise to no one when the announcement was made in assembly; bush telegraph had seen to that. Everybody had known for weeks that the photographer was due and some people even claimed – wrongly as it turned out – to know the date. So it was already public knowledge that after the rehearsal on Friday morning the lottery would take place. They had to wait until Friday to find out who would be in it.

Friday involved a great deal of standing about in a chilly damp wind on the lawn in front of the school. In the centre of the lawn stood a long curved row of eighty chairs, with a row of benches behind them and a row of tables behind that. One after another the classes stepped forward to take their places. On the chairs sat the sixth form with the teachers in the middle and the Headmistress in the very centre. In front of them the second years knelt upright, the most uncomfortable position of all, and right at the front sat the first years, cross-legged and trying not to show their knickers. Because they were only first years people thought that they were too young to care.

The third years stood on the grass behind the sixth form and staff, the fourth year stood behind them on the benches, and at the back the fifth forms teetered on the tables. Symmetry was all. The tallest in every group stood in the middle, the shortest at the sides, and so it was that Jenny and Margery found themselves facing each other across the grass at opposite ends of the third year, and Jenny was remembering what Margery had said last week: 'I bet it will be one of us.' There was a very good chance that it would be, one chance in four, but if it were, Jenny would be the one. Jenny was on the left, the end that the camera started from.

The entrants for the lottery met at the back of the sports pavilion after lunch; Jenny from the third year, one from the second year, one from the fourth and one from the fifth; all the left-hand tail-enders, except for the first year who were considered too young to be trusted, and the sixth who were above such things. Glenda Alcott, the fifth former, was there before them, holding her blue felt school hat in which lay four tightly folded pieces of paper.

'Now then,' Glenda said, 'three of these are blank and one carries the Black Spot. Whoever draws the Black Spot is the one who changes ends. As soon as the camera is pointing to the middle you leave your place and run round to the other end of the line. You know you'll get into a row afterwards. Are you prepared to risk it?'

The other three nodded solemnly.

'All right, then. Draw your papers.'

Madeline Enderby from the second year drew first, then Jenny, then Dawn Fuggle from the fourth and that left one paper in the hat for Glenda and she took it out last of all.

Madeline, Dawn and Glenda looked at each other before they looked at their papers, smiling but grim, as if they had been drawing lots to see who should go to the guillotine, but Jenny just stared at her folded paper, remembering what Margery had said: 'I bet it will be one of us. I have a feeling.' Margery had had feelings before, and they had come true. She had had a feeling before the carol concert last year, that she would be singing the descant in *Adeste Fideles*, and when Susan Beale lost her voice just before they were due to start it had been Margery who was called out to take her place. Then she had had a feeling about the geometry exam that everyone had been so worried about before Easter. 'I have a feeling there won't be an exam,' said Margery, who had done no revision, and on the morning that it was due to take place, Miss Ogden's briefcase, containing the papers, was stolen on the train.

'I have a feeling Cranmer House won't win the acting prize this year,' Margery said, the day before the drama competition, although Cranmer House were a dead cert, and sure enough, on the day, Cranmer went to pieces and fluffed their lines and missed their cues and the cup was awarded to Becket House. Margery and Jenny were in Becket.

Margery's feelings always seemed to involve misfortune for someone, Jenny sometimes reflected, but you couldn't blame Margery for that. *She* hadn't given Susan laryngitis, or nicked Miss Ogden's briefcase. Margery hadn't nobbled the entire cast of Cranmer's play.

'Open your papers,' Glenda said, and Jenny unfolded the little wad in her hand. She hardly needed to look; she knew that it would be her paper that bore the Black Spot.

'You can't back out now,' Dawn said, half envious, half relieved, when Jenny continued to stare at the paper in her palm.

'Remember what I said,' Glenda was admonishing

her. 'Wait until the camera's half-way round in case you're still in shot, then run like hell.' Madeline gasped. She was only a second year. It seemed to her a very desperate thing that grown-up Glenda should say 'hell'.

'And another thing,' Glenda said. 'Don't tell anybody else who's won, except you, Jenny. You must appoint a liaison officer. If you're going to be feeble and come down with something at the last moment you must let us know before Monday lunchtime, so that we three can draw again.'

Jenny knew that there was no chance that she would come down with anything or Margery would have mentioned it, but she had to do what Glenda said, just in case. 'Will you be my liaison officer?' Jenny asked Margery, who showed no surprise when Jenny silently handed her the Black Spot.

'No need,' Margery said. 'If anything happens to you I'll run instead.'

'But you'd have to swap ends,' Jenny said. 'It doesn't work if you run the other way. You don't show up at all.'

'That won't be hard,' Margery said. 'People will think it's you anyway. They usually do. Actually,' she added, 'I have a feeling I may have to do it.'

'Why, am I going to drop dead before Monday?' Jenny snapped. Suddenly she felt that she had had enough of Margery and her feelings.

'Only joking,' Margery said, but Jenny had turned away with an angry flounce. During country dancing that afternoon, she chose Diana Sullivan for her partner, leaving Margery to the mercies of Galumphing Gertie the Games Mistress, who always stomped in enthusiastically to help out anyone who didn't have a partner, and at the end of the afternoon she went straight home alone instead of waiting for Margery who was in a different set for maths.

On Monday morning she made herself especially tidy, as demanded, for the photograph. Rumour had it that school photographs were always taken on Mondays so that even the scruffiest girls might look half-way presentable before they went downhill during the week.

Waiting in the form room for assembly they preened and checked each other out, even though there was the whole morning and lunch to get through before it was time for the photograph, so Jenny had only just noticed that Margery was not in the room before Miss Shaw appeared at the door and beckoned her out.

'Jenny, dear,' Miss Shaw said, as they stood in the corridor, 'I wanted a word with you before I told the others – I know Margery is a very special friend of yours.'

Jenny did not have feelings, not the way Margery did, but she knew what was coming.

'Margery had an accident yesterday,' Miss Shaw said. 'She was out for a drive with some family friends and the car door wasn't properly shut. Margery was thrown out into the road when they took a bend too sharply. She's in hospital. I'm afraid she's badly hurt.'

Jenny, excused assembly, went to sit in the cloakroom and listened to the swarming sound of rubbershod feet as class after class converged upon the hall. The Headmistress must have made an announcement – perhaps they had all said a prayer for Margery's recovery – for at break the news was all round the school. Glenda Alcott came to find Jenny.

'You needn't run if you don't want to,' Glenda said, kindly. 'We'll understand.'

'I'll be all right,' Jenny said, 'Margery wouldn't want me to back out,' but she wasn't too bothered by what Margery would have wanted. All she knew was that if she had the photograph to worry about she might not have to think of Margery herself, lying in the hospital. 'A coma,' Miss Shaw had said. 'Severe head injuries.'

While they were all lining up after lunch, to go out on to the field, Glenda sought her out again.

'Listen,' she said, 'someone told me – someone who *knows* –' she added defiantly, 'that they do it twice, just in case anyone does run.'

'Margery had a feeling they'd do that,' Jenny said.

'The first time they don't run the film. Then if you leave your place you get caught and sent back and you don't dare try it again when they go for the take,' Glenda said. 'That's how they did it at my brother's school. They did it last time we had one here, too, but I didn't realize why. I was only a first year, then.'

If it had been Glenda alone who'd said it, Jenny would probably have doubted, and panicked, and spoiled her chance by running too soon, but as they stood there, tier upon tier, as they had on Friday, she looked across that great curve to the place where Margery ought to have been standing, and did not move. And Margery and Glenda had been right. After the camera had swept round, and while they all stood there frozen and smirking, the little photographer blew his whistle, said, 'All right, ladies, let's do it once more, to make sure,' and redirected the camera, on its tripod, towards Jenny's end of the line. He sounded his whistle again to warn them that he was ready to start and very slowly the camera began to turn a second time. Jenny thought how sinister it looked, clicking round on its

plate, but the first time she had counted the seconds until it seemed to have reached the Headmistress, slap in the middle of the curve, and now, when the moment came, she took a step backwards, turned and began to run.

She hadn't thought before about what it would be like behind the curve. The backs of the fifth years, standing on their tables, reared eight feet above her, blotting out the sun; a palisade of legs, a swathe of skirts, a battlement of heads. The curve seemed endless, for she couldn't *see* the end of it, and the camera was so far ahead of her. In her mind's eye she could see that, the little black eye, inexorably turning, and she ran faster, racing her hidden adversary on the other side of the curve.

Three yards from the end of the line she slipped. The grass was damp where it had lain all day in the shade, her foot skidded from under her and, as she was off-balance already, leaning forward for the final effort, she fell flat, heavily, and lay there winded, all the air slammed out of her lungs. She thought she was going to die, but suddenly she was able to breathe again and scrambled to her feet. But it was too late to run on. As she rose upright the wall of backs relaxed, there was a surge of muted laughter and conversation. The camera had got there first, the photographer had won and the photograph was over. Glenda Alcott, who had seen her leave and had, of course, been able to see also that she had not arrived at the far end, jumped down from the table and hurried round to find out what had happened.

'Did you fall? Bad luck. Hey, don't cry,' Glenda said, when she found Jenny weeping on the grass. Madeline and Dawn, the other tail-enders, were not so charitable.

'If you couldn't do it you might have said, and one of us could have run,' Madeline grumbled.

'I tried. I did try,' Jenny wept.

'Jenny has something on her mind,' Glenda said, severely, and the other two, remembering what it must be, became all at once very serious.

Jenny's mother came up to the school at the end of the afternoon, to meet Jenny and take her home. Jenny was far too old to be taken to and from school, but her mother had something to tell her. Margery had died at just after two o'clock, while they were having the photograph taken.

Everyone at school, girls and teachers, was kind and sympathetic to Jenny – until the photographs arrived, and then the storm broke, for there was Jenny, standing on the left-hand side of the picture, and there, in all her guilt, at the far end, was Jenny again, looking a little dishevelled and blurred, as though she had moved at the wrong moment.

'It isn't me,' Jenny kept saying.

'The truth, if you please,' said first Miss Shaw and then the Headmistress. 'Are you going to tell me that you didn't leave your place?'

'Yes, I did,' Jenny said. 'I did go, I did run round, but I never got there. I fell over.'

She was, as promised, severely dealt with; barred from this and banned from that, and everyone despised her for not admitting to what she had done, when the evidence was there in black and white, for anyone to see; except for three people. Glenda Alcott, Madeline Enderby and Dawn Fuggle had all seen her leave her place, had all been watching the far end to see her arrive, and they alone knew that she had never got there. Lesley Wilson, the girl who was standing next but one at the end of the line and who had, on the day, been at the very end, to start with, said, 'Of course you were standing next to me. I felt your arm. Only I thought at first it was Margery – I mean, it should have been Margery, shouldn't it?'

Glenda borrowed a magnifying glass and they studied that indistinct little figure at the right-hand end of the photograph. 'It *could* be you,' she said, finally. What she didn't say, and what they were all thinking, was, 'It could be Margery.'

'She said if anything happened to me she'd be there in my place,' Jenny said. 'She had a feeling.'

This is why Mrs Sanderson keeps her school photograph in a drawer instead of hanging it on the wall beside her husband's. Even now, forty years later, she can't bring herself to explain.

Old Money

*I*t couldn't happen now. If we found it now we'd throw it away without a second thought – well, perhaps one second thought. Money's still tight, but . . . ten pence . . . it wouldn't be the end of the world.

The point is, though, in 1956 ten pence was two shillings, and although two shillings wasn't a fortune it was still a fortnight's pocket-money. Look at the next ten pence piece you come by. If it's an old one, more than twenty years old, it won't say ten pence on the back, it will say two shillings, and the two shilling piece we got from Mr Tate back in 1956 was old even in those days. It didn't have the Queen's head on it, or her father's, George VI. The head belonged to *his* father, George V, an elderly man with a little beard. It was very worn down and discoloured, but you could just make out the beard, and in any case, we recognized him at once. George V came to the throne in 1910 and died in 1936, but there were still plenty of coins around with his head on them. Victoria turned up sometimes, too.

Gary said he reckoned that Mr Tate had probably had the coin since 1910 anyway. He was only joking, but when we thought about it afterwards we began to wonder if it wasn't the simple truth.

Mr Tate lived farther down the street in a corner house, and everyone said he was a miser. We knew all about misers from comics. They were bitter and twisted and cruel to orphans; also they wore fingerless mittens and hoarded their money in bags with £ signs on, rather as burglars wore striped sweaters and carried bags marked S W A G. Gary's Uncle Timothy was a burglar but he wore dungarees and looked just like a mechanic, which is what he was in his spare time. When he was inside, Gary's mum said he was working up north which, in a way, was true; Durham Gaol.

Mr Tate didn't dress the part either, and wore a hard blue suit. His gloves were tan leather, with fingers, but although he went to work every day, no one seemed to know what he did for a living. His house was shabby and unpainted – although that was nothing unusual in our street – and when he went to the Corner Stores for groceries he never bought more than yesterday's bread and cheap cheese. And he looked miserable, which is where the word comes from, I suppose. A miser is miserable in spite of having money. We were miserable a lot of the time, too; from not having it.

But that Saturday we did have money; two half-crowns – five shillings – oh, all right, twenty-five pence, which Gary Sutton's mum had given him to buy a jar of mustard pickle and some potatoes from the Corner Stores. Mr Tate was ahead of us, buying his bread and cheese which he paid for – we saw him – with a two shilling piece. We saw it because Mrs Goldman looked at it very hard before she put it in the till.

'What's wrong? It's a perfectly good one,' Mr Tate said testily. He said everything testily, as if he expected to be contradicted.

Mrs Goldman held it up to the light and we noticed how black it looked, but it sounded OK when she rang it on the counter and put it in the till. Mr Tate had been scowling across the counter at her, but as the till drawer closed he suddenly smiled, raised his hat, which he hadn't taken off when he went in, and almost bowed out of the shop.

'Must have been drinking,' Mrs Goldman said, half to herself. 'Now, what can I do for you boys?'

'A-jar-of-mustard-pickle-and-ten-pounds-of-good-King-Edwards,' Gary recited.

'What d'you mean, *good* King Edwards?' Mrs Goldman demanded, heaving herself round the counter to reach the potato sack. 'When has your mother ever had a bad potato from me, young man?'

The spuds and pickles came to two and elevenpence halfpenny – just short of fifteen p if you want to know – and Gary handed her the two half-crowns. In return Mrs Goldman gave him a halfpenny and a two shilling piece, the very two shillings that Mr Tate had just given *her*. We were ready to swear to that, afterwards.

She was glaring something awful while she was holding out the money, because Gary didn't take it at first. He looked hard at the two bob, and I looked, too. It *seemed* OK, but it was very black, as if it had been dipped in something that had started to make it change colour.

'It's a perfectly good one,' Mrs Goldman snapped, exactly as Mr Tate had done. We jumped. Mrs Goldman always grumbled at us but that was only force of habit. We never did anything to offend her – unlike Bobby Daniels – and she often gave us broken biscuits. But now she looked really angry, angry and frightened, as though she couldn't wait for us to go. Her hand, with the two coins in the palm, was shaking, and the halfpenny chattered against the two bob bit.

Gary picked them up and dropped them in his

pocket, we took a handle of the shopping bag each and went out of the shop in a hurry. As we left we heard Mrs Goldman call out, as she usually did, 'Goodbye, boys. See you soon!'

'She's changed her tune,' I said. Gary shrugged, moodily. He was slouching and the shopping bag dipped annoyingly on his side, so that the lumpy King Edwards banged against my legs.

'Quit shoving!' Gary snarled, when I jerked at the bag to level it out.

'What's eating you?' I said. Gary had been in a perfectly good mood five minutes before. Now he was scowling, but not angrily, almost as if he was trying not to cry; the same expression he wore when Mr Carter whacked him at school. It was a look that got him accused of dumb insolence and whacked again. He drew his eyebrows together and glared at the ground, while the King Edwards knocked dents in my left leg.

He didn't tell me what was eating him, but he was my mate. I couldn't let him suffer in silence (this is something you only learn to do as you get older) so I kept on at him all the way up the road.

'What's the matter? It wasn't old Ma Goldman, was it? Did Old Tate put the Evil Eye on you?' I didn't know what the Evil Eye was, but catching Mr Tate's eye was usually enough to make you wish you'd been looking the other way.

'Shurrup,' Gary growled, and gave the shopping bag a violent shrug. I felt the edge of the pickle jar bite into my ankle.

'Carry it yourself, then!' I yelled, and letting go of the handle I stormed off ahead of him. I half expected him to shy a King Edward at me and my neck muscles tensed, but instead he called out, 'No, Brian! Wait!'

It wasn't so much a call as a howl. I looked round. Gary was standing in the middle of the pavement looking as miserable as an abandoned dog. I could almost see his drooping tail. There was no way I could leave him there. I went back, picked up the dangling handle, and we walked on.

'Sorry,' Gary muttered.

'What's the matter?'

'I don't know.' He finally looked me in the eye. 'I feel horrible.'

'Ill? You got a pain?'

'No . . . just horrible.' There was a tear on the side of his nose.

We were level with his front door by then. There weren't any front gardens in our street so we went straight in; as straight as we could, that is. Gary's brother was mending his bike in the hall and a clothes horse hung with airing sheets blocked the doorway of the living-room. Gary's sister had the treadle sewing machine out in the middle of the room and his mum was ironing in the kitchen. You couldn't take more than three steps in any direction and there were babies and toys underfoot.

Gary usually trod his way through this maze like a cat stepping round broken glass on top of a wall, but today I distinctly saw him tread on a teddy bear and kick his little sister, though I couldn't be sure whether he did it on purpose or from carelessness, but we left a trail of wailing babies in our wake. Instead of stopping to comfort them as he normally did he just kept going, barging between obstacles until we reached the kitchen table, where he dumped the shopping bag.

'Got the pickles?' his mum said. She could see the potatoes spilling out of the overturned bag. 'Got the change?'

Gary delved into his pocket and dropped the two coins on the table. And smiled. In that second his whole mood changed, his frown vanished, his shoulders straightened. 'Two and a ha'penny, all present and correct,' he said. His mother leaned over and eyed the two bob bit suspiciously.

'Is that a dud?'

'No, just dirty.'

'Put it in the tin, then.'

Gary's mum kept her loose change in a cocoa tin on a shelf above the coke boiler, so that the money in it was always slightly and mysteriously warm. Gary reached it down and looked inside.

'Can I have my pocket money?'

His mum slammed down the iron.

'*Already?*'

'I haven't had last week's yet.' They enjoyed this exchange regularly on Saturdays, so Gary was quite cheerful about it. That was why I was watching him. Only minutes ago he had acted as if he had been told that he had no more than weeks to live, now he was grinning as usual, hands in pockets, ready to take on all comers.

'What's in the tin?' his mum said.

'Two and six, two threepenny bits and three pennies,' Gary said. 'Give us the half dollar, eh, Mum?'

'You're joking,' his mum said, flatly, although of course he was. 'Take the ninepence.'

'Oh Mum. It's *two weeks*.' He was looking at the two shilling piece we'd got from the shop.

'Are you sure?'

'Would I lie?' He turned up his eyeballs, all holy.

'OK, take the two bob. But don't tell your dad.' Officially Gary had ninepence a week, not a shilling. The extra threepence was always a matter for negotiation, or bribery.

Gary meticulously dropped the odd halfpenny into the tin, put it back on the shelf, scooped up the two bob and we zipped out of the back door.

'What d'you say?' Mrs Sutton yelled after us.

'Ta,' said Gary. Anyone would think she'd kept the two shillings and given him the halfpenny. He was right down in the mouth again, dragging his feet as we crossed the Suttons' yard and went through the gate into the back lane. He shoved his hands deeper into his pockets and kicked at a stone. I thought he must have been putting on an act for his mum, because now he looked as miserable again as he had when we came in off the street.

'Come on,' I said, 'let's go up the rec.'

'I don't care where we go,' Gary said, but he plodded after me, head down, and I heard his heels dragging in the dirt.

I couldn't understand it. Gary had a temper, like the rest of us, but he wasn't moody, never sulked, and if anything was bothering him he talked about it – to me at any rate. After all, I was his best mate. But today he wasn't talking, he never said a word all the way to the rec, though I thought he might say something when he saw who was there ahead of us.

The rec was a couple of scrubby grass acres which in summer baked so hard that you could understand how people made bricks with mud. You could break an arm falling over on it and where a long drop was involved, necks were at risk. A pair of swings stood in one corner, with a slide which was useless for sliding *down* because most people walked *up* it, and a see-saw with deep pits under each end where generations of feet had dug into the earth. Suspended upside down from the crossbar of one of the swings was Trevor Passmore. If he'd been hanging by the neck we wouldn't have objected, but he was hanging by his knees; when he saw us he swung himself down and strutted towards us.

We stood in awe of Trevor Passmore, partly because he was a lot bigger than us, and partly because he said that underpants were sissy and refused to wear any. He was tough. We had to believe it, because of the underpants and because he kept telling us so, but he wasn't a bully. He nagged.

'Bet you can't walk down to Woolworth's with your eyes shut,' he would taunt us. 'Bet you can't climb over the fence on to the railway. Bet you can't stand on your head for half an hour.' There was no point in telling him that we didn't much want to do any of these reckless things; he just kept on at us until we tried, and failed, and then he nagged some more, to prove his superiority.

Now he came up to us and said, 'Bet you can't hang upside down from them swings.'

Gary stared at him mournfully and started to walk on, but Trevor dodged in front of him. 'Yer scared. Yer scared. Bet you can't hang upside down from them swings. Bet you can't. Bet you can't.'

'Go and chase yourself,' I said. I said it because Gary hadn't. It was usually Gary who retaliated when Passmore got going, but Gary, sunk in gloom, just kept scuffling over the scorched grass, head down, shoulders hunched.

'Bet you can't. Bet yer scared, bet you wouldn't *dare* hang upside down from them swings,' Passmore intoned, lolloping round us like an incompetent wolf. 'Bet you can't, bet you, betcha, betch.'

At last Gary raised his heavy head, gave Passmore a long, serious look like a man who has received his death warrant and therefore has nothing more to dread, and wordlessly changed direction towards the swings. When he reached the hard asphalt pad where they stood he looked up at the crossbar – he might have been a condemned criminal staring at the gallows – and dragged his hands out of his pockets.

'Hold that for us,' he said, and dropped into my hands the contents of his trouser pockets. Then with one bound he was swarming up the support of the left hand swing. But I wasn't looking at him. I wasn't looking at anything. Just standing upright seemed to require a terrible effort. There was a leaden feeling at the back of my head, not a pain, but a dreadful heaviness, and I knew there was no hope.

If you've never felt like that, I can't explain it. I just knew, in that instant, that there was no point in doing anything, ever again, that nothing mattered; and I knew that I would always feel like this, for ever, until I died, and that wouldn't matter either, because I was nothing. I despised myself for not understanding it sooner.

Up above, Gary was dangling, head down, yelling insults at Passmore. I turned my eyes upward to watch him. Poor Gary. I felt like weeping. Didn't he *know* it was pointless, that whatever he did, and however well he did it, it was all meaningless? With a final jeer, Gary gripped the crossbar with his hands, swung upright and lowered himself to the ground. Passmore, thwarted, growled some kind of grudging congratulation, but Gary brushed him aside and pranced over to where I was standing.

'Not bad, eh? You can't half see a long way up there. Give us me bits and pieces.'

His voice seemed muffled, dull, and the words made no sense. I didn't expect them to. Nothing made sense. Why was I alive?

'Wake up!' Gary bawled, cheerfully. 'Give us me things!'

He held out his hands and with an immense effort I dropped into them all the objects he had given me to hold so that they would not fall out of his pockets; a gnawed stub of pencil, his Boy Scouts badge, a button off his jacket, half a hacksaw blade and two coins – an Irish penny and the two shilling piece.

Gary's hands closed over his possessions.

'That was brilliant!' I said. 'Shurrup, Passmore, you lost your bet.'

'It's nothing,' Gary said. The sad, sick look was back in his eyes. Passmore was taking his defeat like a man, bobbing up and down and trying to shake hands, but Gary just sighed and turned away. I knew how he felt.

I knew how he felt. Then I realized *why* I knew how he felt. Gary was walking away, dragging his feet again. I turned my back on Passmore and ran after him.

'Gary!'

He looked round drearily and didn't answer.

'Lend us two bob.'

I thought I was in for an argument and was trying frantically to think of a reason why I so suddenly needed money, but Gary simply held out his hand with the coin in it.

'Take it,' he said. 'Keep it. Go on. I don't want it any more.'

'No,' I said, 'you don't,' and I flicked it out of his palm with my fingernail, so fast I didn't have time to feel it. The coin spun away into the grass and Gary shot after it.

'What'd you do that for?' he yelled. 'You stupid nit! That's *two* weeks' money, that is.'

'Wait!' I grabbed his sleeve. 'Don't pick it up.'

'You want a knuckle sandwich?'

I was so relieved I nearly hugged him. 'Listen,' I said, 'why did you give it to me?'

He stopped and stared. 'You said "Lend us two bob".'

'I know, but why *did* you?'

'Did what?'

'Let me have it.'

'You're my mate.'

'That's not why,' I said. 'Go on, it isn't, is it? *Is it?*' I
sounded like Passmore.

Gary stopped and thought. 'I didn't want it,' he said,
at last. 'I didn't want anything. I wished I was dead.'

'Wished?'

'No . . . I just couldn't understand why I was alive.'

'I know,' I told him, 'and nor could I, while you were
on that swing – while I was looking after your things.'

Gary gaped at me. 'While you were holding my
money . . .'

The two bob was lying in front of us, on a patch of
bald earth.

'Don't touch it,' I said. 'When did you start feeling
like that?'

'When you gave it back to me, just now.'

'No, before that.'

'In the kitchen.'

'Before that.'

'In the shop.'

'When Mrs Goldman gave you the change.'

'Remember how miserable *she* was?'

'Hang about,' I said. 'Who gave it to her?'

'Old Tate,' Gary said. We looked at each other. 'You
can't get much more miserable than that.'

'Yes,' I said, 'but he wasn't miserable once he'd got
rid of it, was he?'

We sort of crept up on the two bob and stood
watching it. What *was* that blackness on it?

'He must have had it for years,' Gary said. 'Imagine,
if it made *him* feel like it made us feel. All the time.'

'Leave it there,' I said, as Gary stooped to retrieve it.
'Don't touch it.'

'Two shillings!' Gary squawked. 'Get out of it!'

'You know what'll happen if you pick it up,' I warned him.

'Perhaps we imagined it.' But he let it lie there.

'Spend it quick, then,' I said. 'Get rid of it.'

Gary looked shocked. 'I can't do that. Someone else will get it.'

'Yes,' I said, 'but they won't have it long. No one has money for long.'

'Old Tate does. Suppose some little kid got hold of it and put it in a piggy bank?'

'I wonder what Old Tate's doing now,' I said. 'Hey, what say we test it.'

Gary was prodding the coin with a twig.

'You feel anything?' I asked him, anxiously. He shook his head.

'What do you mean, test it?'

'We could give it to someone we don't like – just for a bit – just to see what happens. *Then* we could get rid of it . . . when we're sure.'

'Someone we don't like . . .' Gary was looking thoughtful. 'Passmore?'

'He's not *that* bad,' I said. 'Bobby Daniels?' To be honest, I couldn't think of anyone I disliked enough to make them go through what we'd been through.

'What about Old Carter?'

Of course; Mr Carter. And somehow, doing it to a teacher didn't seem quite so unfair. I mean, there wasn't much Mr Carter didn't know about unfairness.

'How shall we do it?'

'I'll ask him to look after my money on Monday.'

'Yes, but *how*? How do we get it to him – without carrying it?'

You won't believe how we did it. Gary stood guard over the two shillings while I went home for the coal tongs, a paper bag and some string. We picked up the coin with the tongs, dropped it in the bag, tied the neck with string and left a long end dangling. Then we tied the end to Gary's twig and walked back, holding the bag at arm's length. We looked very stupid and we didn't care. The bag spent the rest of the weekend in Gary's outside lav, on top of the cistern, out of harm's way.

On Monday morning we risked being late so as to arrive after everyone else, unobserved. Even so, we got a funny look from the caretaker when we came belting across the playground trailing the paper bag on the end of its string along the ground behind us. We had to pretend we were fooling about and kept yelling, 'Heel, Rover! Good dog! Sit!' but we weren't fooling, no way. On Sunday night we'd tossed up – the Irish penny – to see who would have to handle the coin long enough to take it up to Mr Carter's desk and hand it over. I called heads and it came up tails which was only fair, really. It *was* Gary's money, but he looked pretty sick, after registration, when he carried it to the front and laid it on Mr Carter's desk, even though we'd put it in an envelope.

I saw Gary swallow hard as he said, 'Please, Sir, will you look after this for me till dinner time?' and then he swallowed again, even harder, as Mr Carter took the envelope and shoved it in his pocket.

We had wondered if there would be a sudden dramatic change, but Mr Carter usually looked like a wet weekend anyway, and today was no exception. Even with the money in his pocket, he just went on looking like a wet weekend.

We lined up for assembly after that, and we were half-way through *Praise my Soul the King of Heaven* before Gary nudged me and nodded in Mr Carter's direction. In assembly the teachers sat on chairs alongside their classes, while we sat on the floor, and they always sat bolt upright, looking stuffed. Mr Carter wasn't bolt upright this morning, he was slumped forward with his head in his hands. We couldn't see his face and we didn't want to. When we all stood up at the end and filed out he stayed where he was, until Miss Lewis, from the third year, walked over and touched him on the shoulder. Gary and I were going out of the door by then, and Gary glanced back over his shoulder, to give me a meaningful look.

Miss Lewis took us for double maths, afterwards, then we had break, then history with Mr Bryce and English with Mr Carter. I don't think we'd ever before looked forward to an English lesson so eagerly.

It was due to start at 11.45, but it was ten to twelve before the classroom door opened and Miss Lewis walked in. No one complained. We all liked Miss Lewis better than Mr Carter, but Gary put up his hand and said, 'Please, Miss, what's happened to Sir?'

He had to ask.

We had to know.

'Mr Carter is feeling unwell,' Miss Lewis said. That didn't surprise us, but a sort of ripple ran through the class, teachers being regarded as durable and generally indestructible, except for the real softies who only lasted a term anyway.

A horrid thought struck me.

'He hasn't gone home, has he?' Good grief! If he'd left the premises – with the two bob –

'I don't see what business it is of yours, Brian,' Miss Lewis said, 'but, no, he has not.'

He must be in the staff room, then, and we could just imagine him sitting there, slouched, despairing, head in hands. We knew how he was feeling.

As soon as the dinner bell rang we hurried to the staff room, but before we got there I happened to glance out of the big window in the corridor that overlooked the front drive. At the end of the drive was Mr Carter, just turning right, into the street.

We were forbidden to leave school without permission, but we didn't stop to think about that. Without saying a word we were off, out of the end door – we didn't dare even then to use the front door, next to the Head's office – raced across the grass in front of the school, and out of the gate.

Mr Carter was well ahead of us but not walking very fast. One didn't walk fast, we knew, feeling as he must be feeling. We assumed he was heading for the bus stop, as he usually did at home time, but instead, when he got to the crossroads, by the garage, he turned left.

'Where's he off to?' Gary said, breathlessly. 'What's down there? Maybe he's going to the pub.'

There was a pub down that street, The Green Man, but Mr Carter kept right on past it, head down, shoulders hunched, and we realized he was heading for the station – only he wasn't. When he reached the station approach he crossed over it and went on, up on to the railway bridge.

'Where *is* he off to?' Gary said again. Now we were crossing the station approach, and we could see Mr

Carter's figure up ahead of us, outlined against the sky as he reached the highest part of the bridge; and then he stopped.

Gary stopped too. 'Oh God!' he said, and broke into a run, and I ran after him, for up there on the bridge Mr Carter had got one knee up on the parapet and was just drawing up the other beside it.

'Sir!' I was so frightened my voice had become a breathy squeak. 'No! *Sir!*'

Then a train went under the bridge, an express that wasn't stopping at the station, and Gary and Mr Carter vanished into a boiling cloud of steam, deceptively white and stinking of sulphur. When it cleared I saw, as I came up alongside, Gary holding Mr Carter by the belt of his raincoat, and Mr Carter climbing down off the parapet. He dusted his knees mechanically, and looked down at Gary.

'What do you want?' he asked, as if Gary's sudden arrival was the final straw, and he muttered under his breath, 'No peace. Even in my last hour, no peace . . .'

'Oh, Sir.' Gary was as frightened as I was, but it was a desperate moment. 'Oh, Sir, can I have that two bob you were keeping for me, Sir?'

Mr Carter reached into his pocket, drew out the envelope and handed it to Gary who took it by one corner, pinched in his fingernails.

Mr Carter looked slightly stunned, and shook his head like someone whose ears are full of water. 'Right,' he said briskly, and clapped his hands. 'Back to school. Can't think why we're hanging about here, can you?' and he strode off, whistling, without another glance at us.

Gary laid the envelope on the parapet.

'It was worse for him,' he said. 'It must be terrible for grown-ups. Think of Mr Tate.'

'What are we going to do with it?' I said, 'spend it?'

'We *can't*,' Gary said. 'We *can't* let it get loose. I mean, we could give it to Hitler or Stalin, people like that, but we can't just let it go. *Anyone* might get hold of it.'

I'd been thinking of perhaps putting it in the missionary box at Holy Trinity, with the vague idea of letting it leave the country, but that wouldn't solve the problem. I suddenly understood what people meant when they talked about someone turning up like a bad penny.

And so Gary performed the noblest deed of his life. He took the two bob bit, two weeks' pocket money, and dropped it in the canal. Two bob? What's ten p? I hear you ask. Well then, allowing for inflation, see how you'd feel about setting fire to a fiver.

Right. Now you know what it meant to Gary to chuck that two bob away. But he had to do it. Knowing what we did we couldn't have lived with our consciences if we'd let someone else get hold of it. Of course, for the next couple of weeks I shared my pocket money with Gary – but that came later. When we went home that afternoon Mr Tate was out on the pavement in his shirtsleeves, painting his front door bright red.

'Just a moment, lads,' he said, as we went by. I think it was the first time he'd ever spoken to us, but we stopped, out of curiosity as much as anything.

'Do you remember, on Saturday,' he said, 'you came into the corner shop just after me? I paid for some groceries with a two shilling piece, and Mrs Goldman is ready to swear that she gave it to you two as change.' He looked at us hopefully. 'You don't still have it, by any chance?'

I felt Gary jump. No doubt he felt me do the same. 'No, sorry,' he said, and added, unblushingly, 'we must have spent it.'

'Was it special, then?' I couldn't help asking.

Mr Tate looked sentimental, quite a feat for a face that had only ever looked sour. 'It was the first money I ever earned,' he said. 'I took it home to give to my mother, but she said, "No, Charles, keep it for good luck," and I've had it in my waistcoat pocket ever since. Not always the same waistcoat, ha ha,' he said. It may well have been his first joke. 'I can't think how it came to be mixed up with my loose change.'

'I'm sorry you've lost it,' Gary said.

'Can't be helped,' Mr Tate said, shrugging. He looked amazingly cheerful, in spite of his loss – or because of it for, as we very well knew, there was nothing amazing about it. I've often wondered since if he ever realized exactly the kind of luck his first wages had brought him. I've also wondered what his first employer could have been like, although I think I can guess.

Nule

The house was not old enough to be interesting, just old enough to be starting to fall apart. The few interesting things had been dealt with ages ago, when they first moved in. There was a bell-push in every room, somehow connected to a glass case in the kitchen which contained a list of names and an indicator which wavered from name to name when a button was pushed, before settling on one of them: *Parlour*; *Drawing Room*; *Master Bedroom*; *Second Bedroom*; *Back Bedroom*.

'What are they for?' said Libby one morning, after roving round the house and pushing all the buttons in turn. At that moment Martin pushed the button in the front room and the indicator slid up to *Parlour*, vibrating there while the bell rang. And rang and rang.

'To fetch up the maid,' said Mum.

'We haven't got a maid.'

'No, but you've got me,' said Mum, and tied an old sock over the bell, so that afterwards it would only whirr instead of ringing.

The mouse-holes in the kitchen looked interesting, too. The mice were bold and lounged about, making no effort at all to be timid and mouse-like. They sat on the draining board in the evenings and could scarcely be bothered to stir themselves when the light was switched on.

'Easy living has made them soft,' said Mum. 'They have a gaming-hell behind the boiler. They throw dice all day. They dance the can-can at night.'

'Come off it,' said Dad. 'You'll be finding crates of tiny gin bottles, next.'

'They dance the can-can,' Mum insisted. 'Right over my head they dance it. I can hear them. If you didn't sleep so soundly, you'd hear them too.'

'Oh, that. That's not mice,' said Dad, with a cheery smile. 'That's rats.'

Mum minded the mice less than the bells, until the day she found footprints in the frying-pan.

'Sorry, lads, the party's over,' she said to the mice, who were no doubt combing the dripping from their elegant whiskers at that very moment, and the mouse-holes were blocked up.

Dad did the blocking-up, and also some unblocking, so that after the bath no longer filled itself through the plug hole, the house stopped being interesting altogether; for a time.

Libby and Martin did what they could to improve matters. Beginning in the cupboard under the stairs, they worked their way through the house, up to the attic, looking for something; anything; tapping walls and floors, scouring cupboards, measuring and calculating, but there were no hidden cavities, no secret doors, no ambiguous bulges under the wallpaper, except where the damp got in. The cupboard below the stairs was full of old pickle jars, and what they found in the attic didn't please anyone, least of all Dad.

'That's dry rot,' he said. 'Thank God this isn't our house,' and went cantering off to visit the estate agents, Tench and Tench, in the High Street. Dad called them Shark and Shark. As he got to the gate he turned back and yelled, 'The Plague! The Plague! Put a red cross on the door!' which made Mrs Bowen, over the fence, lean right out of her landing window instead of hiding behind the curtains.

When Dad came back from the estate agents he was growling.

'Shark junior says that since the whole row is coming down inside two years, it isn't worth bothering about. I understand that the new by-pass is going to run right through the scullery.'

'What did Shark senior say?' said Mum.

'I didn't see him. I've never seen him. I don't believe that there is a Shark senior,' said Dad. 'I think he's dead. I think Young Shark keeps him in a box under the bed.'

'Don't be nasty,' said Mum, looking at Libby who worried about things under the bed even in broad daylight. 'I just hope we find a house of our own before this place collapses on our heads – and we shan't be buying it from the Sharks.'

She went back to her sewing, not in a good mood. The mice had broken out again. Libby went into the kitchen to look for them. Martin ran upstairs, rhyming:

> 'Mr Shark,
> In the dark,
> Under the bed.
> Dead.'

When he came down again, Mum was putting away the sewing and Libby was parading around the hall in a pointed hat with a veil and a long red dress that looked rich and splendid unless you knew, as Martin did, that it was made of old curtains.

The hall was dark in the rainy summer afternoon,

and Libby slid from shadow to shadow, rustling.

'What are you meant to be?' said Martin. 'An old witch?'

'I'm the Sleeping Beauty's mother,' said Libby, and lowering her head she charged along the hall, pointed hat foremost, like a unicorn.

Martin changed his mind about walking downstairs and slid down the banisters instead. He suspected that he would not be allowed to do this for much longer. Already the banister rail creaked, and who knew where the dreaded dry rot would strike next? As he reached the upright post at the bottom of the stairs, Mum came out of the back room, lugging the sewing machine, and just missed being impaled on Libby's hat.

'Stop rushing up and down,' said Mum. 'You'll ruin those clothes and I've only just finished them. Go and take them off. And you,' she said, turning to Martin, 'stop swinging on that newel post. Do you want to tear it up by the roots?'

The newel post was supposed to be holding up the banisters, but possibly it was the other way about. At the foot it was just a polished wooden post, but further up it had been turned on a lathe, with slender hips, a waist, a bust almost, and square shoulders. On top was a round ball, as big as a head.

There was another at the top of the stairs but it had lost its head. Dad called it Anne Boleyn; the one at the bottom was simply a newel post, but Libby thought that this too was its name; Nule Post, like Anne Boleyn or Libby Anderson.

Mrs Nule Post.

Lady Nule Post.

When she talked to it she just called it Nule.

The pointed hat and the old curtains were Libby's costume for the school play. Martin had managed to stay out of the school play, but he knew all of Libby's lines by heart as she chanted them round the house, up and down stairs, in a strained, jerky voice, one syllable per step.

'My-dear-we-must-in-vite-all-the-fair-ies-to-the-chris-ten-ing, Hullo, Nule, we-will-not-in-vite-the-wick-ed-fair-y!'

On the last day of term, he sat with Mum and Dad in the school hall and watched Libby go through the same routine on stage. She was word-perfect, in spite of speaking as though her shock absorbers had collapsed, but as most of the cast spoke the same way it didn't sound so very strange.

Once the holidays began Libby went back to talking like Libby, although she still wore the pointed hat and the curtains, until they began to drop to pieces. The curtains went for dusters, but the pointed hat was around for a long time until Mum picked it up and threatened, 'Take this thing away or it goes in the dustbin.'

Libby shunted up and down the stairs a few times with the hat on her head, and then Mum called out that Jane-next-door had come to play. If Libby had been at the top of the stairs, she might have left the hat on her bed, but she was almost at the bottom so she plonked it down on Nule's cannon-ball head, and went out to fight Jane over whose turn it was to kidnap the teddy-bear. She hoped it was Jane's turn. If Libby were the kid-napper, she would have to sit about for ages holding Teddy to ransom behind the water tank, while Jane galloped round the garden on her imaginary pony, whacking the hydrangea bushes with a broomstick.

The hat definitely did something for Nule. When Martin came in later by the front door, he thought at first that it was a person standing at the foot of the stairs. He had to look twice before he understood who it was. Mum saw it at the same time.

'I told Libby to put that object away or I'd throw it in the dustbin.'

'Oh, don't,' said Martin. 'Leave it for Dad to see.'

So she left it, but Martin began to get ideas. The hat made the rest of Nule look very undressed, so he fetched down the old housecoat that had been hanging behind the bathroom door when they moved in. It was purple, with blue paisleys swimming all over it, and very worn, as though it had been somebody's favourite housecoat. The sleeves had set in creases around arms belonging to someone they had never known.

Turning it front to back, he buttoned it like a bib round Nule's neck so that it hung down to the floor. He filled two gloves with screwed-up newspaper, poked them into the sleeves and pinned them there. The weight made the arms dangle and opened the creases. He put a pair of football boots under the hem of the housecoat with the toes just sticking out, and stood back to see how it looked.

As he expected, in the darkness of the hall it looked just like a person, waiting, although there was something not so much lifelike as deathlike in the hang of those dangling arms.

Mum and Libby first saw Nule as they came out of the kitchen together.

'Who on earth did this?' said Mum as they drew alongside.

'It wasn't me,' said Libby, and sounded very glad that it wasn't.

'It was you left the hat, wasn't it?'

'Yes, but not the other bits.'

'What do you think?' said Martin.

'Horrible thing,' said Mum, but she didn't ask him to take it down. Libby sidled round Nule and ran upstairs as close to the wall as she could get.

When Dad came home from work he stopped in the doorway and said, 'Hullo – who's that? Who. . . ?' before Martin put the light on and showed him.

'An idol, I suppose,' said Dad. 'Nule, god of dry rot,' and he bowed low at the foot of the stairs. At the same time the hat slipped forward slightly, as if Nule had lowered its head in acknowledgement. Martin also bowed low before reaching up to put the hat straight.

Mum and Dad seemed to think that Nule was rather funny, so it stayed at the foot of the stairs. They never bowed to it again, but Martin did, every time he went upstairs, and so did Libby. Libby didn't talk to Nule any more, but she watched it a lot. One day she said, 'Which way is it facing?'

'Forwards, of course,' said Martin, but it was hard to tell unless you looked at the feet. He drew two staring eyes and a toothy smile on a piece of paper and cut them out. They were attached to the front of Nule's head with little bits of chewing-gum.

'That's better,' said Libby, laughing, and next time she went upstairs she forgot to bow. Martin was not so sure. Nule looked ordinary now, just like a newel post wearing a housecoat, football boots and the Sleeping Beauty's mother's hat. He took off the eyes and the mouth and rubbed away the chewing-gum.

'*That's* better,' he said, while Nule stared once more without eyes, and smiled without a mouth.

Libby said nothing.

At night the house creaked.

'Thiefly footsteps,' said Libby.

'It's the furniture warping,' said Mum.

Libby thought she said that the furniture was walking, and she could well believe it. The dressing-table had feet with claws; why shouldn't it walk in the dark, tugging fretfully this way and that because the clawed feet pointed in opposite directions? The bath had feet too. Libby imagined it galloping out of the bathroom and tobogganing downstairs on its stomach, like a great white walrus plunging into the sea. If someone held the door open, it would whizz up the path and crash into the front gate. If someone held the gate open, it would shoot across the road and hit the district nurse's car, which she parked under the street light, opposite.

Libby thought of headlines in the local paper – NURSE RUN OVER BY BATH – and giggled, until she heard the creaks again. Then she hid under the bed-clothes.

In his bedroom Martin heard the creaks too, but he had a different reason for worrying. In the attic where the dry rot lurked, there was a big oak wardrobe full of old dead ladies' clothes. It was directly over his head. Supposing it came through?

Next day he moved the bed.

The vacuum cleaner had lost its casters and had to be helped, by Libby pushing from behind. It skidded up the hall and knocked Nule's football boots askew.

'The Hoover doesn't like Nule either,' said Libby. Although she wouldn't talk to Nule any more she liked talking *about* it, as though that somehow made Nule safer.

'What's that?' said Mum.

'It knocked Nule's feet off.'

'Well, put them back,' said Mum, but Libby preferred not to. When Martin came in he set them side by side, but later they were kicked out of place again. If people began to complain that Nule was in the way, Nule would have to go. He got round this by putting the right boot where the left had been and the left boot on the bottom stair. When he left it, the veil on the hat was hanging down behind, but as he went upstairs after tea he noticed that it was now draped over Nule's right shoulder, as if Nule had turned its head to see where its feet were going.

That night the creaks were louder than ever, like a burglar on hefty tiptoe. Libby had mentioned thieves only that evening, and Mum had said, 'What have we got worth stealing?'

Martin felt fairly safe because he had worked out that if the wardrobe fell tonight, it would land on his chest of drawers and not on him, but what might it not bring down with it? Then he realized that the creaks were coming not from above but from below.

He held his breath. Downstairs didn't creak.

His alarm clock gleamed greenly in the dark and told him that it had gone two o'clock. Mum and Dad were asleep ages ago. Libby would sooner burst than leave her bed in the dark. Perhaps it *was* a burglar. Feeling noble and reckless he put on the bedside lamp, slid out of bed, trod silently across the carpet. He turned on the main light and opened the door. The glow shone out of the doorway and saw him as far as the landing light switch at the top of the stairs, but he never had time to turn it on. From the top of the stairs he could look down into the hall where the street light opposite shone coldly through the frosted panes of the front door.

It shone on the hall-stand where the coats hung, on the blanket chest and the brass jug that stood on it, through the white coins of the honesty plants in the brass jug, and on the broody telephone that never rang at night. It did not shine on Nule. Nule was not there.

Nule was half-way up the stairs, one hand on the banisters and one hand holding up the housecoat, clear of its boots. The veil on the hat drifted like smoke across the frosted glass of the front door. Nule creaked and came up another step.

Martin turned and fled back to the bedroom, and dived under the bedclothes, just like Libby who was three years younger and believed in ghosts.

'Were you reading in bed last night?' said Mum, prodding him awake next morning. Martin came out from under the pillow, very slowly.

'No, Mum.'

'You went to sleep with the light on. *Both* lights,' she said, leaning across to switch off the one by the bed.

'I'm sorry.'

'Perhaps you'd like to pay the next electricity bill?'

Mum had brought him a cup of tea, which meant that she had been down to the kitchen and back again, unscathed. Martin wanted to ask her if there was anything strange on the stairs, but he didn't quite know how to put it. He drank the tea, dressed, and went along the landing.

He looked down into the hall where the sun shone through the frosted glass of the front door, on to the hall-stand, the blanket chest, the honesty plants in the brass jug, and the telephone that began to ring as he looked at it. It shone on Nule, standing with its back to him at the foot of the stairs.

Mum came out of the kitchen to answer the phone and Martin went down and stood three steps up, watching Nule and waiting for Mum to finish talking. Nule looked just as it always did. Both feet were back on ground level, side by side.

'I wish you wouldn't hang about like that when I'm on the phone,' said Mum, putting down the receiver and turning round. 'Eavesdropper. Breakfast will be ready in five minutes.'

She went back into the kitchen and Martin sat on the

blanket chest, looking at Nule. It was time for Nule to
go. He should walk up to Nule this minute, kick away
the boots, rip off the housecoat, throw away the hat,
but . . .

He stayed where he was, watching the motionless
football boots, the dangling sleeves. The breeze from an
open window stirred the hem of the housecoat and
revealed the wooden post beneath, rooted firmly in the
floor as it had been for seventy years.

There were no feet in the boots; no arms in the
sleeves.

If he destroyed Nule, it would mean that he *believed*
that he had seen Nule climbing the stairs last night, but
if he left Nule alone, Nule might walk again.

He had a problem.

They Wait

'I don't like getting up in the dark,' Jenny said.

'The clocks go back tomorrow night,' Mum said. 'The mornings'll be lighter then.'

'But the evenings'll be darker,' said Mark.

Jenny said, 'I don't like going out in the dark with all those little things that squeak.'

'Mice?' said Mum, trying to button up Jenny's coat and not listening properly.

'No, not mice,' Jenny said. 'They fly.'

'Do hold still, Jen.'

'You've buttoned a loose bit of my neck into my coat,' Jenny complained.

'Well, what do you expect, wriggling about like that?'

'Flying mice,' said Mark.

'Bats,' said Mum. 'That's what you hear at night. You don't want to be afraid of bats.'

'Bats are flying mice,' Mark said. '*I* can't hear them squeak.'

'I know they're bats. That button's in the wrong hole,' Jenny said. 'Can *you* hear them squeak?'

'I'm much too old,' said Mum, who usually got quite cross if you thought that she was any kind of old. 'But when you're little you can hear all sorts of things that grown-ups can't. Anyway, there aren't any bats at this time of year.'

Jenny said, 'Can I *see* things that grown-ups can't?'

Mum was getting restless because the hands of the

kitchen clock were pointing to half past eight, and you could never be sure with that clock. It might be half past by now, but it could as easily be quarter past, or worse, twenty to nine. She said, 'Yes, I expect so, especially you – you're always seeing things. Do get a move on.'

'No I'm not,' said Jenny. 'Look, you've put your shopping bag on the Major's chair. It's right on his lap.'

Mum lifted the basket on to the table. 'See what I mean?' she said to Mark, over Jenny's head. Only Jenny could see the Major, and the Other Granny, and Mary Dog. The Major and the Other Granny were obviously people but no one, not even Jenny, was sure about Mary Dog. They had never been able to discover whether she were a person whose name happened to be Dog or a dog whose name happened to be Mary. Whoever she was, she lived under the table and rode a bicycle. The Major sat in a wicker chair and spat out of the window. Other Granny, fortunately, lived outside, in the alley, and never went visiting.

'You'd better hurry,' Mum said. 'It can't be earlier than quarter past.' The clock was very old, and had belonged to Real Granny's granny. Sometimes the hands hurried on the way downhill, rested for a bit at the bottom, and dawdled their way toward the top, so the clock was usually right on the hours, but rarely in between. Mark took Jenny by the mitten and hurried her out.

It was a dull morning, more like January than October, and last night's mist was still hanging about in the alley that led to the bus stop on the ring road. Mark trotted Jenny along the alley-way because she would keep stopping to feel sorry for the poor pale roses, with frostbitten petals, that were still growing hopefully through the gaps in Mrs Callaghan's fence. Jenny could be sorry for anything, even plants. Last summer she had taken pity on a poor hydrangea bud that was smaller than any of the others on the bush by the back door. For months she had tried to fatten it up with butter and sugar and juice squeezed out of old tea-bags, and when it went black and died she had picked it and buried it on the rockery. There was still a little cross of twigs where it lay next to the poor dead beetles and the poor dead flies.

The alley turned right and ran downhill slightly, between the backs of garages, until it came out into the open air again by Churchfield Garden. This was a little plot in the angle of Union Street and the ring road. It was fenced with flat round-headed stones, and there was a path along the edge with flower beds on either side, and a lawn in the middle, with another path running across that, and a long garden bench for people to sit on. Very few people did sit there, so it would have been a useful place to play. Mark was too old for that, but when Jenny got under her feet Mum often said, 'Why don't you go down and play in Churchfield Garden?' but Jenny never would.

'I don't like the people there,' she said.

'Has someone been bothering you?' Mum asked, anxiously.

'Oh no, but they aren't nice, those people. There's a little girl with a funny eye, and an old man with one leg, and an old woman with one tooth, and a lady with no head . . .'

'Oh,' said Mum. '*Those* sort of people. Well, ask the Major to go with you – he'll see them off.'

'The Major doesn't go out,' said Jenny. 'Anyway, he wouldn't like them either.'

Jenny would not even cross the garden by the centre path, as Mark did, even when they were late, so every morning it was Mark who ran catercorner to wave down the school coach, while Jenny galloped round the long way, on the pavement.

Mark saw her safely on board, waved goodbye, and then stood back to wait for his own transport. He was too old to be allowed a free journey to school. Either he had to catch the service bus, or, if he were lucky, he might get a lift from Tim's dad, if Tim's dad happened along first, in his car. Although the mist had dispersed here, on the edge of town, he could see that it must be still quite thick out in the country, so he was not too worried when he heard the church clock strike the three-quarters. If he were late for school he could blame the National Bus Company. Tim was going to be late, too, but he could only blame his dad, and Mark, knowing Tim's dad, thought that probably this was not a very safe thing to do.

The clock that he could hear was in the tower of Holy Cross, several streets away. There had once been another church, closer to hand, but Mark had never seen it. It had stood by the burial ground until it was bombed in 1942, which was why the little park was called Churchfield Garden, and the roads on the council estate were all named after it: St Michael's Close, Church Walk, Rectory Drive and The Glebe. Jenny and Mark lived in Church Walk, and Mark knew that their house was just about where the east end of the old church had been, St Michael and All Angels. Jenny did not know that, and cared less. She still had not realized that names meant something, and thought that they were just useful noises. If their road had been called

Coathanger Walk, or Sock Street, she would not have thought it strange. No one who kept friends with a major who spat in public and a dog that rode a bicycle could think that *anything* was odd. The Other Granny did things too, out in the alley, but Mum would not let Jenny talk about her any more. So although Jenny passed the garden every day, and had invented all sorts of strange people to live in it, she never realized why it was called Churchfield Garden, and was too young to remember the time when the council workmen had come and moved all the tombstones to the edge of the plot, so that there was room to lay the lawns and the paths.

The bus was very late; perhaps it had hit a sheep out on the road across the common. But Tim's dad was late too. Perhaps the bus had hit Tim's dad. Mark found his feet turning chilly. It was not really a *cold* morning, but that corner always seemed cooler than anywhere else, always in the shadow of the trees that still grew nearby, or the old warehouse on the far side of the ring road. To keep warm he began stamping like a guardsman round the paths of Churchfield Garden, until he heard the bus growling in the distance on the other side of the bridge. Then he ran to meet it at the bus stop, but not until the very last moment. No matter how warm the day, there was always a chilly wind round the bus stop, and that morning it was bitter. Mrs Callaghan and Mrs Carter from next door, who had also come down to catch the bus to work, had walked all the way up to the lamp-post to keep warm, and had to run even further than he did.

In the evening Mark usually arrived before Jenny's coach, because his bus came round by the ring road while the school coach got stuck in the city traffic, so he waited for her, to see her across the busy road, which was kind of him because if she got there first she never waited for him, but crossed the busy road by herself and raced home as fast as she could. To save him waiting for nothing she would go upstairs and flash her bedroom light on and off. As you could see her bedroom window only from the other side of the road, by the bus stop next to Churchfield Garden, he had to cross over to look, although it meant loitering in that mean chill draught, and then stepping out like a lollipop man when Jenny arrived.

But tonight, when he got down from the bus and crossed the road, to Churchfield Garden, he found that he could not see the window at all. Evidently other people beside himself had complained about the wind for now, next to the bus stop, stood a new wooden shelter with a bench inside it and a timetable in a red metal frame, screwed to the outside wall. He stood first on the left side, then on the right, but no matter where he stood he could no longer see Jenny's window. After hopping about from one cold foot to the other for ten minutes, he decided that Jenny's coach could not possibly be this late, and if it were it was just too bad, and set off home. Jenny, of course, was there before him, in the living-room, being sorry for a poor doggy on television.

'Don't be,' he advised her, 'it's the hero. It's bound to be all right.'

'But it's hurt its poor *paws*, and it's lost in the *snow*,' Jenny whimpered.

'Yes, but in a minute it'll rescue a poor little orphan who's buried in a snow drift and someone'll give it a medal. You know it will. It happens every week.'

'But its paws hurt *now*,' Jenny wailed.

'Idiot. It's a film. It's not even a new film. It was made about twenty years ago.'

'Do dogs live for twenty years?'

'Not often,' he said, unwisely.

'You mean, it's *dead*?'

Mark gave up and went to find Mum. She was in the kitchen, frying sausages.

'Had a good day?' she asked.

'It was all right. Jason sat on my sandwiches at break, but he didn't mean to,' Mark said. 'There's a new shelter down by the bus stop.'

'I know. I saw it when I went into the town for the shopping. They'd just finished putting it up.'

'It'll keep the wind off,' Mark said. 'Did you sit in it? Were you the first? You could have officially opened it – you know: I declare this bus shelter well and truly open and may God bless all who sail in her.'

'It doesn't keep the wind off,' Mum said. 'I did sit in it, and it was even colder inside than it was out. It seems to trap the draught.'

Jenny appeared in the doorway, wiping her eyes. 'I sat in it,' she said, 'just to try it out. But it was all damp and shivery, so I came home.'

'It can't be damp,' Mum said. 'It's new.'

'It is damp – like the outside toilets at the old school.' The outside toilets at the old school were one of the reasons that the old school had been closed.

There was no wind at all on Monday, but it was very cold. As usual Jenny was only just in time for her coach, and Tim's dad was right behind it, hooting impatiently, although the coach was not late, he was early. Mark hopped into the back seat, next to Tim. As the car and the coach moved off together, Mark glanced out of the window and saw that someone was sitting in the bus shelter, although Mrs Carter and Mrs Callaghan were standing where they usually did, out on the pavement, smacking their gloved hands together to keep warm.

That evening Mark got off the bus and saw Jenny waiting for him on the other side of the road, under the street lamp. He went after her.

'What are you doing here?'

'I didn't want to wait in the dark.'

'It's not dark, Dumbo.'

'Why's the light on, then?'

'Street lights always come on before it gets dark, don't they?'

'Well, it's lighter under the light than it is *not* under the light,' Jenny argued.

'You should have gone straight home,' Mark said. 'I wouldn't have minded. You've never waited before.'

'I didn't want to pass the bus shelter.'

'Is there someone hiding behind it?'

'There's a person in it,' Jenny said. 'A person who doesn't get on the bus.'

'Well, there isn't a bus to get on,' said Mark. 'Not till half past. Come on home now.'

'That person was there this morning,' Jenny said. 'I saw him from the coach window.'

'I saw him too,' Mark said. 'It's not the same person, nitwit.'

'It is.' Jenny clung to the lamp-post. 'It's the same person and he doesn't get on the bus.'

'There's no one there now,' Mark said. 'I just walked past it, come and look.' He got Jenny in a kind of friendly half-nelson and propelled her towards the bus shelter. 'Look,' he said, poking his head in, and hers too. 'It's empty, isn't it?'

Jenny looked unconvinced and stayed on the pavement. Mark waved his arms about. 'See? Nobody there.'

'Let's go home,' Jenny said, tugging him out again. At either end of the shelter was a little glazed window, so that people inside could see if the bus were coming, and as they turned away Mark saw what it must have been that had frightened Jenny. Some kind of warp in the glass twisted the light in such a way that it seemed as if there were a person sitting inside, but he said nothing, because Jenny saw only the things that she believed in, and no one had told her about the refraction of light.

Thursday was market day, and there was always a long queue of people waiting for Mark's bus in the

mornings. Mark joined the end of it as Jenny's school coach drew away from the kerb, and watched Jenny's small face peering through one of the side windows, toward the bus shelter. There was nothing fearsome about the bus shelter now. The day was bright, with a little sharp wind rattling the dry leaves of the trees in Churchfield Garden, and tossing them in handfuls round the feet of the people at the head of the queue, but it was bright enough for the queue to stand on the pavement, and not so cold as to drive them into the bus shelter. The bus shelter was quite empty – even very very old Mrs Pickles who had rheumatism and ought to have been keeping warm, was standing in the queue – although when the bus came and Mark had settled into his favourite seat, at the back, he could have sworn as he looked over his shoulder that he could see the indistinct silhouettes of two people sitting together at one end of the bench inside the shelter.

His class had football that afternoon, Reds against Greens. Greens won by five goals to three and Mark, in the Greens, scored two of those five goals. Feeling bold and buoyant as he got off the bus, he crossed the road in the cloudy evening light to wait for Jenny in the shelter, for already a sneaky drizzle was trickling out of the sky. He had thought, when he saw it from the opposite pavement, that the shelter was empty, but when he crossed the road he was not so sure. Instead of going in and sitting down he sauntered back and forth along the pavement that glistened now in the light from the street lamp, certain that there *was* somebody in it, someone who could be seen only out of the tail of his eye; as if whoever it was waited until he had passed and then leaned out behind him, withdrawing into the shadows

again as he turned to come back. The obvious answer
was, of course, to go into the bus shelter and look, since
it might be someone he knew; someone from the estate,
mucking about. But it might be some big tough, like
Gary Callaghan or Cynthia Carter, so he contented
himself with walking past, just once more, and then
going to stand under the street light to wait for Jenny.
When the school coach arrived, a few minutes later, he
did not remain where he was but crossed over again and
collected Jenny from the very step of the coach as the
door swung open.

Jenny glanced across the road.

'There's a lot of people waiting for the bus,' Jenny
said.

'Are there?' Mark said, grimly. 'Where?'

'In the shelter,' Jenny said.

'Then let's stop and watch them get on,' said Mark,
and together they sheltered from the rain against the
wall of the warehouse, and watched the real shelter, the
bus shelter, across the street. From this distance he
could see quite clearly that there were people in it, but
he could not see the people clearly. In spite of the
nearby street lamp, and the fact that daylight still
lingered in the road, the inside of the shelter was thick
with shadows, long solid shadows, that seemed to cast
shadows themselves.

The four-thirty bus changed gear on the other side of
the bridge, and as it came over the hump its headlamps
shone full into the bus shelter, and the shadows shrank
into the corners, but the bus did not stop, for no one
wanted to get off, and no one wanted to get on. When its
tail lights had disappeared round the corner, Jenny and
Mark could see that the shelter was still full of people.

'Well, they didn't get on the bus,' Mark said. 'Who *are* they, Jenny?'

'They're the people who don't get on the bus,' Jenny said.

'Can you see their faces? I can't.'

'Oh yes,' Jenny said. 'I know who they are – I've seen them before. There's the man with one leg . . . and the old woman with one tooth . . . and the little girl with the funny eye . . . and the lady with no head . . .'

Mark turned on her furiously. 'You're making it up!' he shouted. 'They're the people you used to see in Churchfield Garden!'

'Yes,' Jenny said, 'and now they're in the bus shelter.'

'Come on home,' Mark said crossly, and pulled her across the road, just missing a baker's van that came unexpectedly round the corner. He let go of Jenny's hand, feeling that it was her fault that they had been nearly run over, and strode along the path that crossed the garden on the corner. To his surprise he found that Jenny was hurrying after him.

'I thought you didn't like crossing the gardens,' he snapped.

'It's all right now,' Jenny explained. 'There's nobody here. They're all in the bus shelter.'

'Who are?'

'The people who don't get on the bus.'

And they were. The people who *did* get on the bus stayed outside on the pavement, queuing in the rain and wind and even snow, all through the winter. They said that the shelter was draughty, and that there was a funny smell about it, and wasn't it *damp*? The bus shelter gradually filled up with rubbish and vandals broke the little windows at either end, and scrawled all over the outside walls, and tore the timetable from its mounting. No one ventured to scrawl on the inside walls. When the clean spring sunshine showed it up in all its desolation, people began to complain that it was an eyesore, and one day the council workmen came with a lorry and took it away.

Mark saw that it had gone one afternoon as he waited for Jenny, and wondered what had happened to the people who *didn't* get on the bus. He thought that perhaps the council workmen had taken them away with the shelter, for these days Jenny played quite happily in Churchfield Garden, and the shelter really was not needed any more for the wind seemed to have died down considerably, but after a while strange rumours began to circulate about something funny in the bus station, down near the left luggage office, and people stopped going there at night, if they could avoid it.

Birthday Girl

My last year at school, we did community service. We didn't have to, it wasn't like being sentenced by a magistrate instead of going to gaol. We volunteered and got sent to dig old ladies' gardens, and paint old ladies' kitchens and fetch old ladies' shopping. It was mainly old ladies. There weren't enough old men to go round, though some of the old ladies had already got through a couple of husbands.

'Women last longer,' said Mrs Harborough, who was arranging it all.

Me, I was sent to an old people's home with my friend Chrissy, and it was a shock. That was mostly old ladies too, and they just sat around all day watching telly in horrible chairs that were supposed to be easy to get up out of, though none of them ever seemed to go anywhere. It was a shock because when Mrs Harborough said an old people's home, I'd been thinking of Golding House at Burgate. When I was little, being old meant ending up like Mrs Galloway at Golding House.

We met Mrs Galloway only once, but we'd known Golding House for years. It was next door but one to my Auntie Margaret and we went to stay with Margaret every summer, right from when we were tiny. Just looking at her address made us think of holidays; Miss M. Gray, Ocean View, 27c Sandy Lane, Burgate, Kent. You couldn't really see the ocean from Margaret's house, but if you'd climbed on the roof you might have spotted the English Channel, because it was right at the end of the road, which really was sandy, especially after a high wind. From the first floor you couldn't see beyond the roofs of the houses along the sea front, but you could look into the gardens either side and into the garden of Golding House, which was huge, because Golding House was huge. Ocean View was even bigger, and that was why Margaret lived at 27c; because it had been divided up into three separate houses. Golding House was still all in one piece, and the sign outside said *Retirement Home*.

Well, you hear awful things about old people's homes and, like I said, the one Chrissy and I went to wasn't too wonderful, but Golding House wasn't like that. It was a really pretty house, in spite of being so big, with balconies and lots of flowers in hanging baskets, and the gravel drive was always kept nice. And at the back it was lovely, with hundreds of roses and apple trees, even though it was so near the sea, and the grass was always cut in stripes, like they do in adverts. There were wooden park benches put out, and the old ladies – there were only ever one or two old men – used to sit out there in the sun and drink cups of tea and play cards. Some of them had drinks you could see through, and I used to think it wasn't fair that they only had water, but my sister Moya said it was probably gin and tonic and why not? I used to remember that when I was trying to cheer up my old ladies. They never got any gin, believe me.

Margaret's place was tall and thin, only being a slice of a house, if you see what I mean, and when they cut it up, her slice didn't get the bathroom, so they'd built on an extension at the back and put a bathroom in that. It wasn't very nice, dank and always chilly; even the white tiles didn't brighten it up, in fact Margaret said they reminded her of a mortuary, and she said that when she could afford it she'd turn the little spare room at the side into a bathroom, and use the extension for storing all the things she had in the spare room – mostly suitcases and old furniture. Moya and I never slept in it; we had a room at the back.

I remember exactly when that bathroom was built. It was the year I was eleven and Moya was seventeen, and as soon as we arrived at Margaret's we went straight up to see it. She'd had it done beautifully, all in blue; even the soap matched; and when the water ran into the bath Moya said it was like the Mediterranean, not that she'd ever been there, but it certainly wasn't like the Channel at the end of the road.

'Baggy me first bath!' Moya said, forgetting she was seventeen, but in the end it was me that bathed first because I went to bed earlier. Moya went out for a walk down the prom, and I heard her go as I was lying there in the nice blue water, pretending it was the Mediterranean. I heard her come back, too, very late, and have words in the hall with Margaret, about the time.

Then she came upstairs, singing under her breath, and crept into our bedroom, and when she saw I was awake she told me that she'd gone all the way along to the fun fair and met this terrific boy, and she'd been walking on the beach with him and watching the moon come up.

I could not see the fun in that, then – I can now – but I was glad she'd met a nice boy because her last one had treated her rotten, and he really was nice, this one, because she married him two years later, and they're still together. How's that, then?

Anyway, the point of all this was that she didn't get her bath till next morning, and being so happy she woke up early, about six-thirty instead of half past ten like usual, and went dancing off to run her bath in her long nightie that looked a bit like a wedding dress. I prefer big T-shirts, myself.

Well, I lay there, listening to the water running, and then it stopped and the cistern hissed and plopped a bit, and Margaret's old clock in the hall began to strike seven, and then there was this most terrible scream, just one, followed by a sort of wail that ran out of breath, half-way. I ran down the landing, slap into Margaret who was coming the other way. She hammered on the bathroom door, yelling, 'Moya! Moya! What's the matter? Open up! Let us in!' and after a moment we heard a lot of scrabbling and the key turned. Margaret threw the door open and there was Moya, leaning against the wall, clutching her nightie like it was a comfort blanket, and pointing.

And we said, 'What is it? What happened?' And she said, when she got her breath back, she said, 'There was somebody in the bath!'

Margaret went straight over and checked the window catch, but Moya said, 'No, it wasn't like that. I ran the water and turned off the taps, and I was just cleaning my teeth when . . .'

'What?'

'I don't know. Something made me look round, and I saw this . . . this . . .'

'*What?*'

'There was someone lying in the bath, just lying there, under the water, on its – her – I think it was a her – on her back, under the water.

'I didn't do anything at first. I just stood here, I mean, I couldn't believe I was seeing anything, and then the clock struck and she – it – she *sat up*, out of the water, and went – like *that*.'

Moya stuck out her arms, like ghosts do in cartoons. 'And then she just disappeared.'

'Walked through the wall?' I said.

'*Nah!*' Moya was feeling better. She made as if to hit me. 'No, she just, well, disappeared, right where she was, in the bath.'

'What did she look like?' Margaret said.

'I dunno, all in white, long fair hair. I didn't really *see*. Oh, it was . . .'

'Awful?' I said. Moya looked surprised.

'No, it wasn't. I wasn't even scared.'

'What did you scream like that for, then?' Margaret snapped. 'You scared *me*.'

'I was startled. I suppose I'd started to be scared, but I wasn't really. She wasn't frightening.'

I was glad when Moya said that because I was already wondering how I was going to bring myself even to go to the loo in there, let alone lie down in the bath. Think of it. Who would I be lying down *with*? But when I went back into the bathroom later I didn't feel a thing, not fright, not anything, and after a day or two I forgot all about it. It was funny. You might have expected to see things in the old bathroom downstairs, the one like a mortuary, but not up here where it was all new and bright and sunny. Margaret never saw anything, either. She wrote afterwards, and said.

The next year I went alone. Moya had gone off to Ibiza with Tony – the boy she met – and his family, and I took the train down to Burgate alone. It was the same day as last year, that is, it was a Friday, we always went down on a Friday, but this year it was Friday 31 July, last year it had been 1 August. I had a funny feeling when I went into the bathroom for the first time, but only because I was expecting to, and only *as* I went in. There was nothing scary about it once I was in there. Margaret had had a shower put in, over the bath, so I used it, and the next day, too, after I'd been to the beach, but it turned chilly on Saturday night and when I woke up on Sunday I thought I'd have a nice hot bath, so I did. I went into the bathroom and turned on the tap, and then went along the landing for my clothes. I was just coming back, down the landing, when the clock in the hall gave a loud click. It always did that a few seconds before it began to strike, and a few seconds was all it took for me to get back into the bathroom, and there she was.

The bath was about half full, and she was lying just as Moya had said, on her back, just under the water, like she was asleep. She was a little girl, with long hair in a plait that had come untied. She was wearing something white, but I couldn't see what because the water was all stirred up around where her feet would have been, with the tap running, and then the clock began to strike, and she sat up.

I wasn't frightened, I wasn't even very surprised, so I didn't scream or hide my eyes and so I saw her properly, which Moya hadn't done. She didn't wave her arms about like a cartoon ghost, she opened her eyes and smiled, and stretched out her hands, just like she was going to hug someone, and then she disappeared; quite suddenly she wasn't there any more, and the bath had nothing but water in it. The tap was still running and the clock had just finished striking.

I still wasn't frightened, but I didn't get into the bath. It wouldn't have seemed right.

When I'd washed I made Margaret a cup of tea and took it along to her room and sat on the bed while she drank it. She looked at me over the cup and said, 'Well, what's biting you, young lady?' and I said, 'I've seen her again.'

'Seen who?' Margaret said. She really had forgotten.

'You know, what Moya saw, last year, in the bath.'

'Are you having me on?' Margaret said. 'You don't look like you've seen a ghost.'

I said, 'I don't *feel* like I've seen a ghost, but I did.'

'If you say so,' Margaret said. 'I've never seen anything.'

Afterwards I went and looked in my diary which had next year's calendar in it, and last year's too. I never know why they put that in, but this time I was glad they had, because there was something to check. Last year Moya had seen – whatever she saw – on the morning of Saturday 2 August. This year I saw it on Sunday 2 August. And Margaret hadn't seen anything in between. I wondered, was our little girl a special August ghost, just showing up on one day a year? I had another year to wait, before I found out, and I often thought about it, although I never said anything, except to Moya. What I thought was, fancy haunting a *bath*.

I was feeling a bit flat when I went down to Burgate the next year – '82 that would have been. Moya had just got married to Tony and moved away, and I had a rotten cold. On Saturday morning, 31 July (I was counting, see) I stayed at home and felt miserable, while Margaret went shopping. It was one of those wet, windy, wintry days you get at the seaside in summer, all the plants knocked flat and trees leaning over. I sat in the back bedroom and stared out across next door's vegetables at the garden behind Golding House, but all the old ladies were inside and I didn't see anyone except a nurse who came scooting out with a coat over her head to fetch in someone's knitting that had been left out on a bench. It was bright red. I'd been looking at it and wondering what it could be.

Then the doorbell rang. I didn't feel like visitors but I thought Margaret might have forgotten her key so I went down to answer it. There was an elderly lady in the porch – not one of the Golding House residents, she wasn't that elderly – very posh, with lovely shoes. I always notice people's shoes.

She said, 'I'm sorry to trouble you. Is your mother at home?'

I said, 'No, but my auntie's right behind you,' and she was, just coming up the path with her shopping. We all went inside and I made tea, while Margaret got out of her wet things and the lady sat in the lounge. She'd started all over again, apologizing for troubling us, but Margaret said, 'No trouble. Just give us five minutes and we'll have a chat.'

The lady was Mrs Pugh and she'd come about her mother. I thought I'd heard her wrong at first because, frankly, she looked too old to have a mother, but it turned out that her mum, Mrs Galloway, lived at Golding House. The point was, she'd always lived in Burgate, all her life, instead of just retiring there, and she'd actually been born at Ocean View.

'Only it was called The Pines in those days,' said Mrs Pugh. 'Look,' she said, 'it's her birthday on Monday. She's eighty-six. We always take her out somewhere, but this time all she wants is to come and have a last look at this place. I'm afraid it may *be* her last chance,' Mrs Pugh said, and looked very quivery.

'Well, of course she can,' Margaret said, 'but what about the rest of the house? I've only got one end of it.'

'I know,' said Mrs Pugh, 'but this is the part she wants to see, she doesn't care about the rest.'

'I'll be at work,' Margaret said, 'but Diana here can do the honours.' She looked at me hopefully, but I'd have said yes anyway.

So that was two things happening on Monday; Mrs Galloway at ten o'clock and before that, at seven o'clock, my little girl. Because, you see, Monday was 2 August this year, and I was sure she'd be there.

This time I was ready and waiting. I set the alarm for six-thirty and long before seven I was in the bathroom, sitting on the floor opposite the end of the bath, with the door open, so as to hear the clock properly. There wasn't any water in the bath this time. I did wonder if there ought to be but I couldn't see that water had anything to do with it. The clock clicked in the hall, and she was there. She didn't suddenly appear, she was just there, lying in her nightie, like she was asleep, and as the clock began striking she opened her eyes, and sat up, and held out her arms. I was right in front of her, this time. It was as if she was holding them out to *me*. I felt so sad when she went, I said, 'Oh, wait. Don't go,' I really did. But she did go; all at once. Not there any more.

Mrs Pugh and Mrs Galloway were punctual too, on the doorstep at ten sharp. I had tea ready, but Mrs Galloway wasn't interested. You could hardly believe she'd be interested in anything, she was so ancient. I mean, I've met people who were eighty-six, and more, but they didn't look as old as Mrs Galloway, and I saw why her daughter was afraid she might not last another year.

She had a stick and leaned on Mrs Pugh, and I went first to open doors. She peered into rooms and said, 'Mmm, *that's* an improvement,' or 'Ha! Never had one of those!' or just, 'Well I'm damned,' which sounded funny coming from an old lady. Then she said, 'Let's go upstairs.'

Mrs Pugh turned a bit pale. 'Oh, Mother,' she said, 'do you think that's wise?' I could see her point. They probably had lifts at Golding House.

'Of course it's not wise,' Mrs Galloway snapped.

'Who cares if it's wise? Might as well break my neck right now as hang on in that glorified morgue next door,' and she dug her stick into the bottom step like it was the foot of Mount Everest.

It took us about five minutes to get her up those stairs. 'It'll be much worse coming down,' she promised us, when we stopped for a rest, half-way. At the top she looked along the landing, sniffed a bit and said, 'In there.'

'The bathroom?' I felt awful. I hadn't thought of her wanting the loo. Margaret still had one downstairs.

'Is it?' she said. 'Not in my day,' and poked the door open with her stick. 'This was our bedroom,' she said.

We followed her in. 'Oh, Mother,' said Mrs Pugh, 'the two of you in here . . . and all those rooms.' Of course, it had all been one house when Mrs Galloway was a girl. It did seem a bit mean sticking two kids in a room that size. I mean, it was fine as a bathroom, but –

Mrs Galloway was prodding about, holding her stick like a metal detector. 'My bed was here,' she said, pointing to the loo. 'And Queenie was by the window . . . for the fresh air.'

A bed. I don't know why I hadn't thought of it before; a bed where the bath was. I said, 'Was Queenie your sister?'

Mrs Galloway turned and looked at me. It was the first time she'd really noticed me, I think.

'My little sister,' she said. 'They put us in here out of the way. We were poor relations. No one wanted to be bothered with us after Father died.'

'Oh, Mother,' Mrs Pugh said again. She never said much else, come to think of it.

'They weren't cruel,' Mrs Galloway snapped. 'I

never said they were cruel. No one ever laid a hand on us – not for any reason,' and I knew that she meant that if they'd never been beaten, they'd never been cuddled, either. 'Poor little Queenie,' she said. Then she looked at me again, hard, and said, over her shoulder, 'You go down again, Olive. I want a word with this gal.'

'Oh, Mother –' She never actually said it, for Mrs Galloway turned right round and gave her such a look, and Mrs Pugh almost ran for it. 'We'll call when we're ready to come down,' Mrs Galloway said. She plonked herself on the edge of the bath and said, 'Well?'

'Well what?'

'Don't be silly,' she said. 'You want to ask me something. Go ahead.'

'Queenie,' I said, 'you and Queenie. Were you twins?'

'No, I was five when she was born, the year the old Queen died. She was named after her, Victoria, but I always called her Queenie. We shared the same birthday, though,' she added. 'Queenie would have been eighty-one today.'

'When did she die, then?' I said, and I meant, what year, because I thought I could guess the day, but Mrs Galloway said, 'On our birthday. I was twelve, she'd have been seven, but she never lived to see it. She had a weak heart. It wouldn't be the same now, I dare say. Blood transfusions, transplants . . . they'd operate. But Queenie, she just sat around, mostly, all pale and quiet. No one was allowed to excite her, not that much excitement ever came our way. Anything was a treat for Queenie. Some friends of my aunt's had promised us a birthday picnic – if Queenie was well enough, because they knew I'd never go without her, and she was so

excited. Just what she shouldn't have been; I don't
wonder if that wasn't what killed her. When I woke up
in the morning she was lying there in bed with her plait
all untied, and I knew she was dead. Because every
morning I'd expected her to be . . . I didn't tell anyone
immediately. Just went over and sat with her until
seven o'clock and the maids started bringing up tea.'

I began to say, 'But wasn't it at seven when – ?' and
stopped. Mrs Galloway gave me another look. I don't
think she could see much, but she could *look*.

'Go on,' she said.

I said, 'I think I've seen Queenie. Me and my sister,
we've both seen her. I saw her this morning, and last
year, and the year before. Always on 2 August, at seven
o'clock.'

'It would have been six, though,' Mrs Galloway said,
half to herself. 'We didn't have daylight saving then. So
that's why I woke up. I just missed her.' She put out her
hand and took mine, and her voice was ever so gentle
now. 'Oh, my dear,' she said, 'how does she look?'

'She looks happy,' I said. 'She's asleep, and then she
wakes and sits up, and holds out her arms, like this. And
she smiles.'

'Is that true? You're not just saying it.'

'It's true,' I said. 'She doesn't frighten us. She's
lovely.'

'Yes, she was lovely, my Queenie,' Mrs Galloway
said. And then she said, 'I always thought she'd died in
her sleep. I'm so glad she lived long enough to know it
was her birthday.

'You know why I'm here, don't you?' she said. 'I'm
not supposed to last out the year, according to the
doctors, but I reckon I might, now I know. Do you think

your auntie would object if I paid her another visit on my birthday, next year?'

'At seven o'clock?'

'At seven o'clock.'

I wish I could say that she did, but the doctors were right and she was wrong. She never did come again, but neither did Queenie. I suppose she didn't need to, any more. When I told Moya about it she said, 'Would you wait that long for me?'

Who's a Pretty Boy, Then?

Rachel's house had a very small garden. The people on the end of the terrace had a big one, round the side as well as at the back, but Rachel's house was in the middle, so there was only a small strip of garden behind, and none at all in front. Once Rachel had travelled right to the top of Debenham's, on the escalators, to where they kept all the furniture and carpets. Some of the carpets were laid out on the floor, as if they were in a real house, and there was one carpet that was as big as Rachel's whole garden; well, almost. Two of those carpets would definitely have been bigger than Rachel's garden.

Rachel's mum could have done with a bit more room because she liked growing things, and there was not much scope for gardening on a carpet, but she made the most of what space there was. Along the back fence, by the alley, there were sprouts and cabbages, with fringes of radishes and spring onions in between, and the lusty rhubarb that was trying to get out, through the palings. In the middle was a grass plot that had to be cut with shears because there wasn't enough to buy a mower for, and down either side were flowers. Mum even had little bushes growing in old buckets, on the concrete up by the back door, and there was a stringy sort of vine that did not look at all well, and that had come over the wall from Mrs Sergeant's.

'For a bit of peace,' said Mum, pruning it tenderly.

So the whole garden was a carpet of grass and plants except for one threadbare patch, the size of a large hearthrug, right next to the house. Nothing grew there.

Mum couldn't understand it. It was a good sunny spot, sheltered from the wind, but it made no difference what she planted, nothing came up. She tried carrots and lettuce first, and when they failed she put in onions, then beetroot, then marrows and finally nasturtiums which are difficult *not* to grow, but by now it was getting late in the year, and nothing was growing anywhere. Next spring she set bedding plants instead of seeds, but after a few days the plants looked poorly and lay down limp. Then she got silly and planted dandelions. 'They'll grow if nothing else does,' she said, but they didn't. Even fireweed would not grow there.

'It must be the drains,' Gran said. 'You ought to get the council to have a look. It might be typhoid.'

'I'd have thought bad drains would be good for plants,' said Mum. 'Ever see a carrot with typhoid?'

Gran sniffed.

By the time they had lived in the house for three years, Rachel's little sister Donna had been born, Gran had moved to Maidstone, Rachel was at the Junior school and Dad suddenly started to be interested in budgerigars. Gran had kept a blue budgerigar called Pip in a cage on the sideboard, but Dad did not approve of birds like that.

'Is it cruel to keep them in cages then?' Rachel asked. She thought it probably was cruel.

'I don't know about cruel,' said Dad, 'but it doesn't look natural to me, a full-grown bird standing on one leg with a bell on its head saying, "Who's a pretty boy, then?" and kissing itself in the mirror. If we have any birds they're going to behave like birds'; and on the bald patch where nothing grew, he built an aviary.

First he put down concrete, and over this went a tall enclosure of wire netting on a frame of battens, in the angle of the house and the garden wall. At one end was a wooden sentry box with perches, where the birds could sleep safe from draughts and passing rats.

'There aren't any rats round here,' said Mum.

'Livestock attracts them,' said Dad, and made all the joints and angles rat-proof. Rachel hoped there would be rats.

At the weekend Dad and Rachel took the bus out past the M2 flyover and spent the afternoon looking in the woods for good sound branches so that the birds would have somewhere to sit, like wild birds, and afterwards they went up on to the downs to find lumps of chalk, essential for healthy feathers. They had a bit of trouble on the way home with what the bus conductor referred to as half a dead tree. 'I ought to sell you a ticket for it,' he said, and there was some unpleasantness with a woman who complained that Dad had tried to put her eye out, but they brought it home safely and it was set up in the flight, which was what Dad called the open part of the aviary.

'Why's it called an aviary, Dad?' Rachel asked.

'Look it up,' said Dad, as he always did when Rachel wanted to know what words meant. She was never sure whether this was because he thought it was good for her to look things up, or because he did not know the answer. She took care not to ask him which it was. This time she fetched the dictionary and learned that the Latin word for bird was *avis*. She was pleased to know some Latin.

For a long time the dictionary had been the only book on the shelf, but now it had been joined by magazines and illustrated books about budgerigars. The birds in the pictures were brightly coloured and when Rachel leafed through the pages her eye was captured by succulent names; Lutinos, Opalines and Satinettes, Cobalts, Cinnamons and Visual Violets; glassy, glossy words with rare flavours. She imagined the dead branch in the aviary brilliant with expensive sweets like a fabulous Christmas tree.

Then the budgerigars arrived. There were six of them and they came in little cardboard boxes with holes in the sides. Dad took them into the aviary and let them loose, then he left, without the birds following him, because he had built the aviary with double doors. There was a space between them which was, he said, the air-lock. Rachel looked up air-lock and decided that he must be joking.

'What are we going to call them?' Rachel said.

'We're not going to call them anything,' Dad said. 'They don't need names. And another thing,' he said, sternly, to Rachel and Mum and Donna who had come out to watch, 'I don't want anyone trying to teach them to talk. These budgerigars are going to be as near wild as tame birds can be. There's going to be trouble if I catch any of them creeping up to me and saying, "Who's a pretty boy, then?" And no wolf-whistles.'

Mum went indoors to give Donna her lunch, but Rachel stayed close up against the wire and watched the budgerigars ('I don't want to hear anyone calling them budgies') exploring their new home, bouncing on the branches and tidying their feathers, investigating seed trays, grit pans and water pots. There was no doubt that they looked much more impressive in their aviary than Pip had done in his cage, but she could not help wondering if they wouldn't be happier with a bell or two, and a mirror.

'They don't need mirrors,' said Dad, 'they've got each other to look at.'

When the birds had settled in they began to purr and chirrup in the sunshine.

'See,' said Dad, 'they can talk to each other. There's no point in making them learn words, those squawks are all the language they need. They mean something.'

'So do words,' Rachel said.

'Not to budgerigars,' Dad said, firmly. 'You can teach a budgerigar to say the Lord's Prayer. You can teach him to sing *God Save the Queen*. You can teach him to count to a hundred backwards, but he'll never know what he's saying. They don't really *talk*, they just copy sounds.'

Rachel remembered Pip, looking sideways into his mirror and saying coyly, 'Who's a pretty boy, then?' He had always sounded as though he knew exactly what it meant, and very pleased with himself; but then, budgerigars usually did sound pleased with themselves, and they looked smug, too. Rachel thought it might be something to do with having no neck.

It was a fine August, that year. Donna sat in her pram in the middle of the grass, and squawked when the birds squawked. She would watch them for hours as they bowed and curtsied, turned somersaults and hung by one leg. Rachel liked spying on them when they went to sleep in the shelter, with their heads turned right round and their beaks buried in their back feathers. It gave her a furry feeling in her front teeth;

little kittens had the same effect, and baby rabbits.

The budgerigars had been in residence for almost six weeks when Dad came home from work one evening in a bad mood. They could tell he was in a bad mood by the way he shut the kitchen door. He always came in through the back gate and paused to have a look at the birds on his way past the aviary, before coming indoors. Tonight he didn't stop in the kitchen; he went straight through to the front room where Rachel and Mum were watching television.

'Own up, then,' he said. 'Who did it?'

'Who did what?' said Mum. 'Keep your voice down or we shall have old mother Sergeant banging on the wall.'

'Who's been at those birds?'

Mrs Sergeant thumped on the wall.

'Have they got out, then?' Mum looked alarmed. 'Rachel, have you been fiddling. . . ?'

'Oh, they're all there,' said Dad, '*and one of them's talking*. Who did it?'

'What did it say?' Rachel asked. She hoped that it had not said hello. She always said it herself as she passed the aviary on her way to school; not to teach them, just to be friendly.

'I say "Good morning, ladies and gentlebirds" when I put the seed in,' Mum said. Rachel was surprised. It was not the kind of joke that Mum went in for. 'Don't tell me that *they've* been saying "Good morning, ladies and gentlebirds" too,' said Mum.

'Stop acting innocent,' said Dad. 'Come out here and listen.'

They went out to the aviary. One of the birds was white, more noticeable than the others and more

sociable. Rachel thought of it as Snowball, although she was careful never to say so. When the white bird saw the family standing round, it flew up to a branch and sidled along, until it was close to the wire.

'Pretty me,' it said.

'Hear that?' Dad demanded. 'Pretty me! I'll give it pretty me. Who's been saying "Pretty me" to that bird?'

'No,' said Rachel. 'I haven't.' She was not quite sure if this was, in fact, what the bird had said. The words had come out muffled and rather subdued, not at all like Pip's self-satisfied croak. She wished it would speak again but it only sat there on its branch, the little wrinkled eyelids crimping up and down.

'If any of those birds says another word, *one* other word, there'll be trouble,' said Dad. He was looking at Rachel.

'I never,' said Rachel.

'I suppose it was Donna, then.'

Donna hadn't even got around to saying ma-ma yet.

'Well, it wasn't me,' Mum said. 'Why don't you sell up and get canaries instead? They don't have much to say for themselves.' She went indoors.

After tea, when Dad had gone to play darts at the Man of Kent, Rachel slipped out to the aviary again. The white bird was still sitting on its twig, next to the wire. Rachel went and stood close, sucking her teeth as Gran used to do with Pip, to indicate that she was ready for a chat. The white bird opened its eyes, and its beak.

'Pity me,' it said, in its sad, hoarse voice. 'Pity me. Pity me.'

Rachel's first thought was, 'Good; it isn't copying anything I've said.' Then she began to wonder who it was copying. Surely no one would deliberately teach a budgerigar to say 'Pity me'? Perhaps Mum had said it without thinking –; people didn't say things like that without thinking. Perhaps the bird had *tried* to say 'Pretty me' but couldn't talk very well? Perhaps Mrs Sergeant had been having a go at it, over the wall.

Rachel sucked her teeth again.

'Pity me,' said the white bird. One of the green budgerigars, there were two of them, fluttered down from the topmost twig and clung with beak and claws to the wire netting. It turned its head sideways to look at her.

'Pity me,' said the green bird.

The two yellow birds clambered up from below. 'Pity me. Pity me. Pity me.' Rachel shivered. She had not noticed that the sun was down below the roofs of the houses in the next street. The aviary was in shadow and she could only just make out the shape of the blue budgerigar, hunched on its perch in the shelter, in silence, while the white, the green and the yellow birds pressed against the netting and repeated dully, 'Pity me. Pity me.'

The next day was Saturday, mild and still, and in the morning the budgerigars swung and fluttered in the aviary with never a word to say. They nibbled at chickweed, honed their beaks on cuttlefish bones and chucked millet seeds about, very busy being budgerigars; but as the day wore on an uneasy silence settled over the aviary. Birds sang in other gardens but the budgerigars fluffed themselves up, drew their spare feet into their feathers and closed their eyes. They looked, to Rachel, not so much tired as depressed. She went over to the netting, carrying Donna, and said, 'Come on, boys, cheer up.'

A yellow budgerigar opened one eye and said, 'Oh, I'm so cold. Oh, I'm so cold.'

'Pity me,' said the white bird. The others ruffled their feathers and were motionless again.

'Cross my heart,' Rachel gabbled, that evening. 'Cross my heart and cut my throat, it wasn't me.'

'None of that nonsense,' said Dad. 'I want a straight answer, yes or no. Did you or didn't you?'

'No!' Rachel yelled. She was shocked. People didn't yell at Dad. 'I never did. Anyway, if I had, I wouldn't have taught them to say things like that. I'd have taught them "Give us a kiss" and – and –'

'Who's a pretty boy, then?'

'Yes. But I *didn't*.'

It was raining on Sunday. The budgerigars stayed in their shelter and looked at the weather with their small eyes half shut, and said nothing all day. Dad was on late turn the following week, from four till midnight, so he saw the birds only in the daytime when it was bright, and they were bright, but it seemed to Rachel that they were not so bright as they had been, and after Dad left for work, wheeling his bicycle away down the alley, she visited the aviary. The birds, that had stopped flying and gibbering, settled on their twigs and shuffled towards her; all of them, all six. They looked furtive and unwell.

'Pity me,' said the white bird.

'Oh, I'm so cold,' said the two yellow birds.

'Pity me.'

'Cold as clay,' said the blue bird that had never spoken before.

'*What?*'

Rachel jumped and turned round. Mum was standing behind her, lips pressed together tight and frightened.

'What did that bird say?'

'I don't know, Mum.' She did know, but she did not want to tell.

'Don't say anything to your dad. I'm going to watch out, this evening. Someone must be coming into the garden after dark and doing this.'

Mum watched every evening that week, and caught no one, heard nothing, even though she kept up her vigil until Dad came home at midnight. By the weekend the birds had stopped squawking and flying from twig to twig. The chickweed withered untouched; the millet sprays hung neglected from the branches. On Saturday morning Dad and Mum and Rachel stood round the aviary and listened to the listless little voices droning,

'Oh, I'm so cold.' 'Pity me.' 'Oh, I'm so cold.' 'Cold as clay.' 'Pity me. Pity me.'

'This is getting beyond a joke,' Dad said, and talked of calling the police.

'Come off it,' said Mum, 'you can't call the police because your budgies are talking daft.'

'You call that talking daft?'

'No, not really, but they aren't damaged, are they? They haven't been stolen.'

'Not damaged? Look at them.'

They all looked at the bedraggled birds, with their feathers poking out at odd angles like bristles on a bottle brush, and their dreary eyes. The white budgerigar, once the most beautiful of all, had pulled out its tail feathers and slouched on its perch with all the grace of an old shuttlecock.

'What could the police do?' Mum said. 'Question them?'

Dad scowled and went to consult his budgerigar books. Later he went shopping and came home with cod-liver oil and fortified seed and a mineral block like a lump of grey Edinburgh rock.

'To cheer them up,' he said.

'They'd probably fancy a nip of whisky, sooner,' said Mum. 'Wouldn't you?'

They had not cheered up by Sunday evening, and on Monday, the last day of October, Dad was back at work. He was on the night shift now, and did not leave home until twenty to twelve. Rachel heard him go, kept awake by the continual opening and closing all evening of the back door, as Mum and Dad took turns to leap out on the intruder; but they didn't catch anyone. When Dad's rear light had turned left at the end of the alley, Rachel crept downstairs. Mum was clearing up, before going to bed, but she sat down at the table when Rachel padded into the kitchen. She sighed.

'I don't know.'

'I'm sorry, Mum. I couldn't sleep. The back door . . .'

'I didn't mean you, it's those blooming budgies. We've been in and out a dozen times this evening, and we haven't heard anyone.'

'I don't think there's anyone to hear,' said Rachel.

'You get along to bed,' Mum said, crossly. 'You'll be having me see things, next.'

Rachel said, 'I don't think there's anything to see, either. I don't think there's anything at all, and only the birds can hear it. Are you going out to look?'

'No,' said Mum. 'Not on your life – and neither are you.'

When Dad came home from work next morning, he found Mum and Rachel standing by the aviary, watching the budgerigars that drooped on their branches.

'Oh, I'm so cold,' said one.

'I shall always be very cold,' said another, 'cold as clay.'

'I shall always be here,' said a third.

'I shall never go away,' said the white bird.

'Pity me.'

'Pity me.'

'No,' said Dad, for the twentieth time. 'No!' he shouted. 'We are not moving. I never heard such nonsense. We're staying here.'

'Right,' said Mum, 'then it's up to you. Either those birds go or I do.'

The budgerigars were sold to good homes and went to live in cages with bells and mirrors. Donna missed them very much, so instead of the budgerigars they got a Hartz Roller canary that lived up to its name by standing on its toes all day and yelling 'Rrrrrrrrrrrrrrr-rrrrr' on a very high note. Dad broke up the aviary and on the place where nothing would grow he put down crazy paving in five different cheerful colours with a little pond in the middle. He called it a patio and to decorate it he bought a plastic orange tree in a pot and a plaster stork to stand by the pond. Rachel didn't much like the look of the patio, but the orange tree did not die, and the stork never said a word.

Grow Your Own

'This year,' said Dad, at the beginning of February, 'we'll have the lawn up.'

'You've been saying that for three years,' Mum said. 'I'll kind of miss it when it goes.'

'This year I mean it,' Dad said. 'This year it's curtains for the lawn.'

'Where shall we play, then?' Andy, who had been slouching with his nose almost in his cornflakes, reared up, bristling. 'You won't let us play in the street. It's not fair. We shan't have anywhere.'

Andy could be depended upon to see the worst side of any situation. Susan, who always took her lead from Andy, put down her spoon, carefully, and prepared to weep, looking round first to see if anyone would notice. Jean, who had heard it all before, went on eating.

'Anyone would think,' Dad said, 'that I was going to pull the house down and put you out on the street. All we are going to do is move the path, dig up the lawn and lay a new one, where the path is now. You'll still have plenty of room to play.'

'All?' Mum said.

'We?' said Jean.

'You'll help, won't you, Jeannie,' Dad said bracingly, but with a pleading look in his eye. 'And you little ones can have a plot each of your own to grow what you like.'

Susan slammed her tear ducts into reverse and beamed. 'Can I grow a tree?'

'A little one.'

'I want to grow a huge tree.'

'The garden's too small for that. A big tree takes too much nourishment from the soil.'

'You said we could grow what we liked,' Andy growled. 'I'm going to grow weeds.'

After breakfast Jean went out with Dad to look at the lawn. It had been a sorry sight when they first moved to the house, and it looked even sorrier now, after three years of Andy and Susan, bicycles, footballs, roller skates and Andy's misguided attempt to light a camp fire and roast potatoes.

Jean carried the trug freighted with stakes and twine. Dad had the retractable tape measure that the little ones were forbidden to touch, because it whipped back into its case like a recoiling rattlesnake. He let it out to its fullest extent, four metres, and prowled about, frowning, occasionally prodding the earth with a gardening cane. Jean drove a stake into the ground wherever he prodded, and then they strung the twine from stake to stake, which reminded Jean of those puzzles where you join up the dots, for when they had finished, the network of twine showed the outline of the new lawn and the route, across the old one, of where the path would be. Dad went into the shed to put away the tape measure on a high shelf, and Mum came down the garden to hang out the washing.

'Having fun?' Mum said, with pegs between her teeth.

'It's going to look nice,' Jean said, loyally. She had said the same thing when Dad planned the alpine garden which was where Andy and Susan had their sand pit, and when he had proposed to put up a rose arch exactly where the washing line went across. From behind a dangling double sheet Andy and Susan appeared, looking suspicious.

'I liked our lawn,' Andy said, mournfully, as if he could only just remember it but would never forget.

'Oh, come off it,' Jean said, 'it's a horrible lawn, all bald and stony. And it's full of dandelions and cats go on it. The new one will be lovely, all green and springy. You won't cut your knees if you fall over,' she added, appealing to their self-interest. She did not mention the fact that even after the new lawn was planted it would be a long while before they could play on it. There would be time enough for that in summer, when Andy got his skates out.

'Where's my bit?' Susan said. 'Daddy said I could have a bit of my own.'

'I don't know. Let's go and ask him – leave that twine alone, Andy.'

' 'snot your twine,' Andy retorted, twanging it, but only while she was watching. She turned her back and went down to the shed with Susan trotting behind.

'Dad? Sue wants to know where she can have her bit of garden.'

Dad was at the back of the shed, inspecting flower pots. He came out and stood in the doorway, considering. 'How about there?' he said, pointing to a modest corner behind the currant bushes. Susan went over to look.

'I don't like this place. There's things in it.'

'What sort of things?'

'With wings.'

'Lots of things in the garden have wings,' Dad said. 'Butterflies, ladybirds, beetles –'

'Beetles have legs.'

'And wings. Come on, Sukie, this is probably the best part of the garden. Lovely soil. And it won't matter if you grow trees down here.' This was because the plot he had earmarked for Susan was far away from everything except the shed. It was also rather shady. Very likely only a tree would grow there anyway. 'As soon as we've got the lawn up you can start digging.'

'I want *that* place.' Susan pointed towards the fence, and a cosy, sunny little nook on the far side of the shed.

'No, you can't have that. I'm going to put the compost heap there.'

'What's a compost heap?'

'We're not going to use peat and artificial fertilizers any more,' Dad said. 'We're going to make our own compost. We'll put all our grass cuttings and potato peelings and tealeaves and weeds in a big pile and they'll rot down into lovely rich soil.'

'Don't you need a bin for that?' Jean said.

'I prefer to do it the traditional way,' Dad said. 'So off you go, Sukie. Behind the currant bushes.'

'But what about the things?'

'If you're going to be a gardener,' Dad said, 'you'll have to get used to *things*.'

In spite of united opposition Dad began digging up the lawn the following Saturday. It looked like a little ploughed field, row after row of gleaming sods, neatly turned. Andy and Susan said nothing but played a pathetically shrinking game on the dwindling patch of grass, until they were huddled together in the very last corner, like castaways marooned on a rock with the tide coming in.

'Right,' said Dad, when the lawn had vanished

entirely, 'we'll leave it like that until spring and the frost
will break it down.'

'Frost?' said Mum. 'If we have another winter like
last one –'.

'There's sure to be a frost before April,' Dad said. 'No
reason why you two shouldn't make a start,' he said, to
the children who were sulking on the rockery. 'Do you
want the spade, Andy?'

'Don't need a spade,' Andy said, kicking the rocks.
'Weeds come up on their own.'

'Don't they just,' Mum said.

Susan was staring wistfully at the place where Andy's
plot would be. 'Can't I have a place where it's sunny?'

'It's mine!' Andy leaped into the centre of his terri-
tory as if prepared to defend it with his life.

'It's only sunny *now*,' Jean coaxed. 'In the morning
your place will get the sunshine.'

Susan retreated a few paces towards the currant
bushes.

'You can't see the house.'

'Yes you can.'

'Not from *my* place. It's round the corner.'

'Oh, go on, swap,' Jean said to Andy. 'You don't
really care which bit you have.'

'I'm not going down by the compost heap. It'll stink,'
said Andy, with some truth.

'But you're not going to grow anything anyway. Oh,
come on, Andy. Don't be so mean.'

'I'm not really going to grow weeds.' Prudently
keeping one foot on the plot to maintain ownership he
spread out like a pair of compasses and grabbed the
spade that Dad had left standing in the earth. 'I'm
going to grow lovely sunflowers,' he declared, for

Susan's benefit. '*Sun*flowers need *sun*. Don't they, Jean? You've got to have *sun* to grow *sun*flowers. I can't grow *sun*flowers down by the stinky old compost heap because there won't be any *sun* there. Poor old Susan. No *sun*.'

'Oh, shut up,' Jean said, aiming a kick at him but taking care not to connect, for fear of further ructions, as Andy began to dig ferociously, like a miner whose mates are trapped by a cave-in. She went back down the path to where Susan was lurking disconsolately beside the compost heap.

So far it was scarcely more than a mole hill and so scanty that you could count the contributions; three orange peels, four days' tealeaves, two banana skins, a melon rind, potato peelings and a glossy aubergine that had secretively rotted at the back of the fridge. From a distance it all shone festively, like a bunch of unseasonable flowers.

'I don't like this place,' Susan whimpered, forlorn among the currant bushes. 'I want to change with Andy.'

'Andy won't change.' While they were talking she could hear the spade chomping energetically into the earth. 'He's already started digging.'

'I shall be sad.' There was a certain amount of threat in Susan's voice but she really did seem to be upset, not just putting it on for an act. Jean surveyed the plot behind the currant bushes. As far as she could tell the only thing wrong with it was the proximity of the compost heap, and as yet, that was much too small to cause offence. Susan could have no idea of what it *would* be like, say in a year's time.

'Don't cry, Sukie. When you plant some flowers it

will be lovely here, too.' Jean went down on one knee beside her little sister and immediately saw why Susan was unhappy. On that eye-level the garden was entirely hidden by the currant bushes and then by the evergreen laurustinus shrubs beyond them. The house was out of sight, too. All that Susan could see when she looked round were two towering, sombre cypresses and the overhanging shed. When the compost heap rose to its full height even the view through the paling fence into Mrs Lawrence's garden next door would be obscured. Jean had never been small enough in this garden to imagine how threatened Susan felt, but she remembered the last house and the last garden where, when she was Susan's age, the sundial had reared above her like something escaped from Stonehenge. She had been so proud of climbing a tree that was, she could see now, not much taller than Dad. Couldn't *he* understand how easy it was to be frightened when you were so close to the ground? Presumably he had once been that size, too.

'I'll tell you what,' Jean said, standing up, 'I'll let you have a bit of *my* garden, up near the house. Would you like that?' Susan nodded, beginning to smile again. 'And I'll have this piece, to make up.'

'Can I grow my tree?'

Jean frowned. Her stretch of the garden was wide and shallow, laid out neatly in rows, tall plants at the back, short ones in front, and Mum said it looked like a school photograph. 'You don't really want to grow a tree. You only said that to annoy Dad.'

Susan giggled and nodded again. That was all right, then. They walked back up the garden together on the crunching cinder path that would soon go the way of the lawn. Round at the side of the house lay a stack of paving slabs bought to replace it. They paused beside Jean's plot.

'Which is my place?' Susan said.

'Here at the side, from the Michaelmas daisies down as far as Mum's roses. You mustn't touch *them*.'

She was very reluctant to give up even a centimetre of her carefully tended plot in exchange for that no man's land behind the currant bushes. The only consolation was that it was far too early in the year to think of planting anything, and that by the time April came Susan, and probably Andy too, would have lost all interest in gardening.

Long before that, though, the new garden began to take shape. Dad dug up the cinder path and laid the concrete slabs. Rain and frost broke up the clods of the old lawn and Jean's hoeing did the rest. By the end of March the site of the new lawn was raked level and the seed sown. By the end of April a fine green mist lay over it, thousands of slender grass blades. In the borders Mum's tulips flared, red and yellow; the Ville de Lyon clematis was swarming up the rose arch although it would not flower until July.

Meanwhile, at the end of the garden, the compost heap was growing too. From that first little offering of fruit and veg it had increased to half a metre in height and Dad had erected an enclosure of boards round it. Jean, sowing neat rows of land cress and lettuces, watched it rise. Its finest moment came in May when the new lawn was cut for the first time. Dad snipped daintily at the tender blades with newly sharpened shears, and collected up the fine clippings to place on the compost heap.

'I love the scent of new-cut grass,' Jean said, sprinkling the clippings over yesterday's discarded cabbage leaves and turnip tops.

'That's decomposition. Grass begins to break down organically as soon as it's cut,' Dad said. 'That's what you can smell.'

All through the summer, as the grass grew longer and stronger, there was a regular harvest of clippings for the compost heap. When Jean went down to water her salads, now she had radishes and spring onions, too, she was aware of it working away silently, turning the grass, the weeds, the kitchen refuse into the lovely rich soil that Dad had promised. Even on chilly days the compost heap felt warm and alive. She was longing for the time when they would remove the boards at the front and with a spade lift out the nourishing earth in dark slices, like Christmas pudding.

Andy's weed garden flourished for a couple of months and then he was given a skate board and forgot all about the pleasures of horticulture. Susan planted a number of interesting stones alongside Jean's tobacco plants and verbena and stuck a lopped branch from the apple tree upright in the middle of her plot.

Sometimes she ventured as far as the currant bushes to see how Jean's vegetables were coming along.

'Can I have a radish?'

'Not yet. Next week, perhaps. What's that you've got there?'

'A mouse.' Susan held it up by the tail. In fact it was two thirds of a mouse.

'Where did you find that?'

'In my garden,' Susan said. 'Do you think it was ill?'

'I should think it had a headache,' Jean said, looking at the corpse. Evidently Mrs Lawrence's cat Dennis had lost his appetite in the middle of a meal. 'Why are you carrying it around?'

'I was going to bury it,' Susan said.

'Chuck it on the compost heap,' Jean suggested. The mouse was swinging unpleasantly close to her face. 'Go on, it'll rot down with everything else.'

'Won't Daddy mind?'

'Ordinary earth's full of things that have died, isn't it?' Jean said. 'I should think that mouse would be very good for the compost.'

Susan made a dent in the latest thatch of grass clippings and laid the mouse reverently in it.

'Now wash your hands,' Jean said. The mouse had not been fresh.

When she came down later with the potato peelings from supper she noticed that the grass was looking rather scattered and the mouse had gone. Presumably Dennis had come back for second helpings.

'*Is* it all right to put meat on the compost heap?' she asked Mum, when they were washing up.

'Meat? What had you in mind, lamb chops? A few spare ribs?'

'Dead mice.'

'Why, have you got more than you can handle?'

'Susan found one that Dennis had left. I told her it could go in the compost.'

'I don't see what harm it can do,' Mum said. 'I've been chucking them on for months.'

'Mice?'

'You know what Dennis is like; mice, birds, fish . . .'

'Where's he get the fish from?'

'Dustbins, I should think. Anyway, it all goes on the heap.'

'Doesn't Dad mind?'

'Haven't told him,' Mum said.

Next time Jean encountered one of Dennis's leftovers which could, she thought, have been a rat, she scooped it up on her trowel and tipped it on to the compost heap, but this time digging a small grave first, among the cabbage leaves. She must have disturbed an air pocket, down there among the lovely rich soil, for as she turned away there came a sound from the compost heap, something between a gasp and a gulp – possibly a soft but satisfied belch.

The first frost of the year came early at the end of September, sharp and unexpected. Susan went out before breakfast to make footprints on the pale sparkling veil that was the new lawn. Jean followed her, shivering slightly, to inspect damage to plants. The low sun slid between the palings of the fence as it rose, leaving stripes of frost across the path where their shadows had lain. There was a broad white band of it where the laurustinus stood and behind the currant bushes Jean's vegetable patch was thickly iced. On the compost heap only a few crystals glittered, already melting, although the sun had not touched it yet.

Jean looked back along the path. The Michaelmas daisies had survived but the chrysanthemums' heads hung dully. The last dahlias were black and late rosebuds drooped where the cold had pinched them. Only the apples shone now in the bright air. Coming down the path Jean had seen her breath steaming, and now she noticed a faint haze above the compost heap, as if

that too were breathing gently in the cold light. The end
of the garden lay in deep shadow and the only thing
high enough to catch the sun was the upper part of the
shed. The bottom part stood in the shadow of the
compost heap and from that shadow, on either side of it,
lay twin pillars of shadow cast by the cypress trees,
straight up and then bent at identical angles as they
crossed the roof of the shed. There was no stir of wind,
they did not move, but as she looked the shadow
between them shifted slightly, as if something had
moved on top of the compost heap.

Jean turned sharply, expecting to see Dennis the cat,
or even a squirrel. Susan would like to see a squirrel.
There was nothing there, but something must have *been*
there for the top of the heap looked disturbed, almost
churned over. All the frost had vanished suddenly,
faster than it could have melted in the chilly sunlight.
She edged alongside the heap and looked over the fence.
How nice if it were a squirrel. But there was no trace of a
squirrel over the fence in Mrs Lawrence's garden, and
no cat. A trail of little cat feet ran across the white lawn
between the rose bushes, but they came nowhere near
the fence, nowhere near the compost heap. Jean stepped back towards the path but as she moved she
knocked against the wooden boards that enclosed the
heap. It wasn't a hard enough knock to dislodge anything, she thought, but the top of the heap shuddered
and little clods and clumps fell away. An old green
potato with sprouts like giant pincers rolled down,
crabwise. From inside the mass came what sounded
like a warm damp sigh. Although there was no wind
a withered leaf and a shred or two of dried grass drifted
to earth.

Back up the garden Susan was hovering near the blasted remains of Jean's frost-bitten plants.

'Can we dig them up now they're dead? Can we put them on the compost heap?'

'If you like.' Jean looked thoughtfully at Susan. She was five. It would be a pity to frighten her for nothing but even so . . .

'Sukie?'

'Mmmm?'

'Have you noticed anything about the compost heap?'

'It's bigger than me, now,' Susan said.

'Anything else?'

'It makes a funny noise.'

'What sort of a noise?'

'Like breathing,' Susan said. 'It's gases escaping.'

'It's what?'

'I asked Daddy. He said it must be gases escaping. Like when you eat too much and go *erp*.'

'Oh, yes. Sure.'

They went shopping that morning, but in the afternoon Susan helped Jean clear the dead plants from her flower bed. Jean cut down the chrysanthemums and separated the roots, ready to store in peat till next spring. It was growing chilly again when they went in, and darkness was falling when Jean looked out of the window and noticed that the trug containing the dead plants was still standing on the path.

She went out to fetch it and set off down the garden to the shed. Already stars were showing and a white moon skimmed the chimney stack. There would be another frost tonight, a hard one.

Jean upended the trug on the compost heap. It was

not only bigger than Susan, now, it was very nearly as tall as she was. As she opened the shed door to put away the trug, it crackled and stirred behind her.

When she looked out of the bedroom window the next morning the world was almost white. Frost lay palest green on the grass and stood thick upon twigs. Across the lawn ran a line of delicate prints from the toes of Dennis the cat, and *up* the lawn, from the direction of the shed, from the direction of the compost heap, lay a long dark track, as if something warm and heavy had passed that way, something that had moved close to the ground.

Jean threw on her dressing-gown and ran down to look, across the patio, down the steps, under the rose arch and along the path. The track on the lawn was scraped clear of frost, littered with dead leaves and bits of grass, potato peelings and dark soil, and where the lawn ended the trail went on, over the frosty rockery and under the hedge, into Mrs Lawrence's garden.

Before she reached the shed she knew that something had changed. The shed stood in full sunshine, right down to the ground, and the only shadows on it were cast by the slender palings of the fence and the two pillars of the cypress trees. There was nothing to obstruct the sunshine any more, for the rampart of boards that had enclosed the compost heap was scattered on the ground, as if something had burst them apart, and the compost heap had gone too, or rather, it had collapsed. On the earth where it had stood, a metre and a half high, lay a little pile of the rich dark soil that Dad had been looking forward to, a scattering of dead weeds and peelings, and chrysanthemum heads, the withered verbena and tobacco plants, a carrot top like an orange button. The rest of the heap was missing.

Moving very slowly, Jean went back up the garden, following the trail of earth and leaves through the frost, across the lawn, over the rockery, towards the hedge. Like the footsteps of Good King Wenceslas it seemed warm to the touch of her bare feet. On the far side of the hedge was another scattering of earth, marring the clean-swept bricks of Mrs Lawrence's patio. Round the corner of Mrs Lawrence's house came Dennis the cat, with an early morning mouse in his teeth. He laid it tenderly upon the ground and patted it with his paw. It did not respond. Dennis reared back on his haunches and took a swing at it, the mouse rose into the air and at the same moment, from behind the dustbin, something lunged out, caught the mouse with a swift clawed swipe

as it began to fall, and withdrew behind the dustbin again. Something growled, a cat-like growl, but Dennis was already in flight, up on the fence with eyes like marbles, fur on end, tail like a bottle brush, all four paws clustered together on one post.

From behind the dustbin came a throaty, satisfied rumbling; not quite a purr. Jean leaned right over the hedge, in time to see a bulky shape trundle from its hideout and head through the long grass towards the lane. It was a dark shape, low-slung, rotund and heavy, and the whispering grass stems closed behind it. It could have been a hedgehog – a hedgehog as large as Susan, but unlike the general run of hedgehogs, it seemed to have acquired a taste for mice.

Welcome, Yule

Probably Emma would not have come to know Mr Jarvis, the new vicar, if someone had not tipped him off that her dad could play the organ. They never discovered who had done it, although Dad did say that whoever it was ought to be hung up by the heels and skinned with a butter knife, which would have been worth watching, but one day the vicar arrived on his motor cycle, without warning. Emma came home from school and found him in the living-room with a cup of tea at his elbow, Mum hovering and Dad cowering.

'I believe you're something of an organist,' said the vicar, to Emma's dad, who was off work with a broken finger. He was a draughtsman at Featherstone's.

'Not at the moment,' Dad said, waving his fat finger like a parsnip in its bandages.

'Well, that won't last for ever,' the vicar said.

'Nor will I,' Dad said, glumly. He hated to be ill, even in one finger. Emma loved it because she was healthy and hardly ever had a day off school.

'It would only be two weeks in three,' said Mr Jarvis. 'There's no music at Holy Communion.' He would not give in. After about an hour, Dad gave in, because his finger would keep him off the keys for at least another month and, as the vicar had said, it was only two Sundays out of three.

Ockney, Cawley and Strang shared one vicar among them. Emma lived in Strang, and the vicar did too, because it was the largest parish. It had a council estate, a factory, and the smallest Woolworth's in England, perhaps in the whole world. On Sundays he buzzed in a bee-line from church to church on his motor cycle; Holy Communion at Ockney, Matins at Strang and Evensong at Cawley. On the following Sunday they each celebrated a different service. Emma thought it was like musical chairs, and wondered what would happen if one of the churches fell down during the week, and the vicar was left stranded with a spare service and nowhere to say it. Churches had fallen down before. On the hill above Strang, between Highmead Estate and Featherstone's Marine Diesel Engines Ltd, lay the remains of St Thomas's Church. Six hundred years ago old Strang village had stood on the hill around St Thomas's, but after the Black Death, which wiped out all but seven of the parishioners, the village moved away and started again in the valley, with a new church, Holy Trinity, which showed no signs of falling down.

Up on the hill, St Thomas's slid gently back into the ground until the grass covered it, and now the local children played on the grassy lumps and bumps that had been the nave and chancel. They preferred it to the council playground where there were swings and slides and concrete pipes to crawl through. Emma herself preferred it. She did not live on the council estate, but she often went up to play at St Thomas's.

'I'm not playing on some old church,' said her cousin Naomi, when she came to stay. 'It's spooky,' Naomi said, before she had even seen it.

'It's not,' Emma said.

'I bet there's ghosts.'

'I've never seen one,' Emma retorted. 'Not up there, at any rate.'

'Where then? Bet you never.'

'Bet what you like. You wouldn't know a ghost if you saw one,' Emma said, and they went off to play in the concrete pipes.

The vicar came to see Dad in July. By September Dad couldn't pretend any longer that his finger was stiff, so all through the autumn he went down to Holy Trinity, two weeks out of three, to play the organ at Matins or Evensong. Mum and Emma, who had never been church-goers, sometimes went along too, to lend him moral support, and often Mr Jarvis visited them to discuss next week's music. Dad found himself playing the organ at choir practices as well, at weddings and funerals, and then suddenly it was November, and the vicar began to talk about Christmas carols.

Winter had come early that year. The vicar stood on the frosty doorstep, staring at the black sky and the burning blue stars, while his breath steamed in the light from the hall, and the hall grew colder and colder. Mum and Emma huddled round the boiler in the kitchen and wished that Dad were brave enough to boot the vicar out and shut the door. At last they heard the roar of his two-stroke as he shot away down the hill.

'One of these nights he'll come off at that bend by the bridge,' Mum said, hopefully, as Dad came back into the hall and shut the door.

'He thinks there'll be snow before Christmas,' Dad said, rushing to the boiler with his purple hands held out in front of him, like a rocket-powered sleepwalker. 'Says he can smell it.'

'All right for some,' Mum said. 'They've got central heating at the vicarage.'

'He wants to go carol singing,' said Dad.

'I can just see that,' said Mum. 'I can just see him belting round the county on his Yamaha, singing "Silent Night" fit to raise the dead.'

'Not by himself,' Dad said. 'He thinks we should all go out with the three church choirs and tramp round Ockney and Cawley as well. Candle lanterns and mulled ale and Jack Pewsey with his clarinet.'

'Jack plays hot jazz,' Mum pointed out.

'I should think we could cool him down enough for a few carols.'

'The weather'll do that,' Mum said.

'It had better. If it's not Jack Pewsey it'll be me with a portable harmonium and four boy scouts to pull it.'

'The Baptists at Ockney have a harmonium,' said Mum. 'It sounds like a string quartet in a drain.'

'I know – I'll go down to the Three Compasses and buy Jack a few pints,' said Dad.

Emma said, 'If you go carol singing, can I come?'

'We'll all come,' Mum said. She turned to Dad who was putting on his parka. 'The vicar wasn't here last Christmas, was he?'

'Came just before Easter. I remember the first time I saw him – lurking under the lich-gate on Good Friday.'

'Then someone ought to tell him about the Waits. He shouldn't upset the Waits.'

The vicar's idea caught on. Everybody in Ockney, Cawley and Strang wanted to go out carol singing at Christmas, although not all of them wanted to go with the vicar. Strang Women's Institute decided to dress up in Olde Tyme clothes and go round with a sled, distributing tea and sugar to the Olde Age Pensioners. Cawley Comprehensive got up a rival scheme involving Christmas puddings, while the Ockney Baptists wheeled out their portable harmonium and began rehearsing on their own account. On still evenings it could be heard even by the nightwatchman up at Featherstone's Marine Diesels. The vicar became concerned by the threat of so much competition and planned a campaign to eliminate it. He called a meeting in the parish room at Strang, to explain his strategy.

He had brought along a map of the three parishes, divided up into zones with red lines and arrows. Emma, looking at it, was reminded of a plan for battle. She could picture Mr Jarvis lying in ambush with his carol singers armed and hidden behind a hedge, waiting for the Ockney Baptists to come wheezing by. The vicar explained what the red lines were for.

'Carol singing starts a week before Christmas. The W.I. are going round Cawley and Ockney on the twentieth and twenty-third, and Strang on the twenty-second. Cawley Comp will be in Ockney on the twenty-first. Strang on the twenty-third, and at home on the twenty-second. Ockney Baptists will be in Strang on the twenty-first, and Ockney and Cawley on the twenty-second and twenty-third. How's that for dovetailing?' said the vicar.

'What about us?' Dad asked.

'Aha,' the vicar said, teeth glistening with satisfaction. 'The united church choirs will be at Ockney on the nineteenth, and Cawley on the twenty-first, but we'll be in Strang on the twentieth. That, you see – if you'll just look at this chart – gives us first crack at Ockney and Strang. No one will have been round before us.'

'And first crack at the collection,' Dad muttered.

'What about the Waits?' Emma asked. She nudged Dad. 'Mum told you to tell him about the Waits.'

Dad looked embarrassed. 'It's not that simple, Em.'

Emma could believe it. The vicar was not the kind of man to listen to things that he did not want to hear, but she was firm. She prodded her father.

'Go on, Dad.'

Dad coughed. 'Er, Mr Jarvis . . . is this absolutely final?' he asked, pointing to the map.

'And foolproof,' said the vicar. 'Why, is there a fly in the ointment? Trust you to find it.'

'Not exactly. It's just that the Waits always sing in Strang on the twentieth. It's St Thomas's Eve, you see . . .'

'Waits? Of course I know it's St Thomas's Eve. What Waits?'

'Waits. You know, the old name for carol singers,' Dad said.

'Ah, yes; Middle English, from Old Norman French *waitier* from the Old French *guaitier* . . . What about them? We've not had any complaints from them?'

'Well, you wouldn't,' Dad mumbled, 'but they might not like it.'

'Who are these Waits? A music society?'

'You could call them that,' Dad agreed.

'If they wanted to book the twentieth, they should have spoken up. I announced the provisional dates ten days ago. No one said anything. Who's their chairman, or secretary, or whatever they have?'

'I don't think they have one,' said Dad. 'They're not an official society, just local people who like to come together to sing carols on St Thomas's Eve. It's a kind of tradition,' he said, lamely.

'They're perfectly welcome to join our band,' the vicar declared, brisk and reasonable. 'I'll say as much on Sunday.'

On Sunday, at Evensong, he announced that the Waits would be very welcome to come carol singing with the united church choirs of Ockney, Cawley and Strang, on the twentieth of December, but not on any other night, and not on their own.

'We don't want clashes between rival supporters,' the vicar said, with a jolly smile. There was an uneasy, almost angry, muttering among the congregation.

'I'll be very surprised,' Mum said, under her breath, 'if anyone from Strang turns out for His Nibs on the twentieth.'

School ended on Tuesday the nineteenth, and that evening Mum and Dad and Emma wrapped up warmly, collected Jack Pewsey, who was Emma's headmaster, and Jack's clarinet, and drove over icy roads to Ockney, where they met the three choirs assembled outside the King's Head, and sang 'O Come All Ye Faithful' by way of a warm-up, before moving on to render 'The Holly and the Ivy' – with particular emphasis on the line about the playing of the merry organ – to the Baptists, practising in the chapel with their harmonium.

Next day, on the morning of the twentieth, Jack Pewsey rang up, in a hoarse voice, to say that the cold air had got to his lungs and he wouldn't be able to play his clarinet in Strang that night.

'Lungs, my foot,' said Mum. 'He doesn't want to upset the Waits, that's what.'

'Sensible fellow,' Dad said, and rang the vicar.

'I think we'll have to call it a day, tonight,' he said, but the vicar rang up the Ockney Baptists and that afternoon the pastor drove over in his minibus and unloaded the portable harmonium at Emma's front gate, just as Dad was coming home from Featherstone's.

'But won't you need it yourselves?' Dad asked, with wan hope.

'Not till Thursday, thanks to Generalissimo Jarvis,' the pastor said, leaping back into the minibus. He was an athletic man. He had unloaded the harmonium single-handed. It took the combined efforts of Mum, Dad and Emma to move it into the garage.

'No luck,' Dad said. 'I'll have to go through with it.' He looked with loathing at the minibus, skidding round the bend by the bridge. 'Why do clergymen drive so badly? I knew this mad monk in Macclesfield – had a Volvo . . .'

'We'll come too,' Emma said, firmly. If the Waits turned out for a showdown with the vicar, she wanted to be there to see it.

They gathered under a starry sky in frozen silence, by the west door of Holy Trinity. The choir from St Mary's Ockney was there, and the choir of Cawley All Saints, but from Strang there was no one but Mum, Dad, Emma and the vicar.

'I see,' said Mr Jarvis, peering into the darkness. 'I see.'

'I doubt it,' said Emma's dad, bold after a couple of whiskies with Jack Pewsey who had claimed that his tubes needed flushing and coughed hollowly to prove it. 'The Waits sing tonight.'

'And people in Strang prefer to go out with the Waits

rather than support their own church choir?'

'No one goes out with the Waits,' Dad said, 'but it's their night, and no one wants to offend them.'

'They had plenty of warning,' the vicar snapped. He turned to the four boy scouts, harnessed like reindeer to the Baptists' harmonium. 'One, two, three – *heave!*'

The choirs moved off, and did not halt until they reached the bridge where Emma's own road went round the corner.

'We'll begin with "Once in Royal David's City",' the vicar announced.

Dad unfolded his camping stool, sat down at the harmonium, and began to play. The choirs began to sing. After they had finished with Royal David's City the scouts went round knocking on doors, while Dad struck up 'Good King Wenceslas'. It was a good carol for a cold night, and the choirs sang vigorously, but at the end of every verse Emma could have sworn that somewhere, not too distant, another choir was singing 'Good King Wenceslas', four bars behind.

'"Oh Little Town of Bethlehem",' the vicar commanded, when they had finished, and they began again. This time there could be no doubt. Somewhere in the streets of Strang, another choir was singing; *not* 'O Little Town of Bethlehem'. When 'O Little Town of Bethlehem' was over, they all paused to listen. Across the frosty rooftops chimed the strains of a carol that Emma had never heard before, but rather liked:

> *'Out of your sleep arise and wake,*
> *For God mankind now hath y-take,*
> *All of a maid without any make;*
>   *Of all women she beareth the bell.*
>   *Nowell, nowell, nowell . . .'*

'It seems we have competition,' the vicar remarked, redundantly, when the carol was over. 'Time we moved on, I think.' He chivvied the scouts back into position and the group slithered over the glittering pavement in the swinging yellow light of the vicar's lantern which he bore before them, on a pole. As they went they heard, apparently from the street beyond the market, a crisp treble voice singing,

> *'Welcome be thou, heaven-king,*
> *Welcome, born in one morning,*
> *Welcome for whom we shall sing,*
> *Welcome Yule!'*

'I know the words,' the vicar said, intrigued in spite of himself, 'but I must confess that the tune is entirely unfamiliar.'

'It's the original, I'd guess,' Dad said, blandly.

They stopped at the corner by the service station. ' "While Shepherds Watched",' said the vicar. In answer, and certainly in the next street, a sturdy chorus of deep male voices broke out.

> *'The boar's head in hand bear I,*
> *Bedecked with bays and rosemary,*
> *And I pray you my masters be merry . . .'*

' "While Shepherds Watched",' bellowed the vicar, so they sang it, while a single voice, sharp as splitting ice, cut through their chorus:

> *'Gabriel from heaven-king*
> *Sent to the maiden sweet,*
> *Brought he this blissful tiding,*
> *And fair he gan her greet.'*

'Move on!' the vicar shouted. 'This is getting beyond a joke. Move on!'

As they approached the deserted market square a light was seen, bobbing up Brewer's Street, above a cluster of dark figures.

'Could this be our friends, the Waits?' the vicar inquired, nastily, and raising his own lantern on its pole, he strode to meet his rivals, while the choir and the harmonium, conductorless, floundered through 'See, Amid the Winter's Snow'. Emma shuffled her cold feet in their cold boots, and stopped singing to hear what would happen. One by one the rest of the choir fell silent as the vicar and the Waits met at last, outside Woolworth's.

'Merry Christmas,' the vicar cried, not at all merry. The Waits stood and faced him, all in a lump. Their lantern shone over their heads, greenish, not glowing.

'I'm sorry it's come to a confrontation,' said the vicar, 'but we gave you plenty of warning. You were cordially invited to join us and there were notices saying as much put up in the church porch, the Post Office, and outside the police station.'

The leader of the Waits, a huge muffled man in a heavy coat, or cloak, stepped forward a pace, but still no one spoke. The vicar stepped back.

'We'd still be delighted,' he said, less certainly, 'if you'd care to join forces, but if not, I really must ask you to move on. It's not as if,' he added, 'you were even singing the same carols as us. Indeed,' he went on, 'I'm not sure that what you are singing *are* carols. I've never heard . . .'

As one man, the Waits moved; forward, sideways, and disappeared. It looked very much as if they had gone into Woolworth's, but that could not have been so, because Woolworth's closed at five-thirty, and it was now twenty minutes to nine.

'Very clever,' said the vicar. 'Most entertaining. I think this has gone far enough. Who are they?'

'Well, we don't know any of them personally,' Dad said, 'but I told you, it's an established tradition. They always come out to sing carols on St Thomas's Eve. John Aubrey mentions having seen them in – sixteen forty-seven, I think it was.'

'John Aubrey? Sixteen forty-seven? Are you trying to tell me – ?'

'That was the year Parliament abolished Christmas, but it didn't make much difference to the Waits. They kept going right through the Commonwealth, much to the annoyance of the vicar,' he added, pointedly.

'This has been going on since *sixteen forty-seven*?'

'Oh, much longer than that,' Mum chipped in. 'I imagine it really got going after the Black Death. When was that? Mid-fourteenth century?'

'*But who are they?*'

'Like I said, we don't really know any of them by name, except for the big bloke with the lantern. He's Will Plowman,' said Dad. 'Always carries the lantern, Will does.'

'Since when?'

'Since thirteen forty-eight, that's when,' Mum said. 'Good old Will. It would take more than Oliver Cromwell to make him miss his carols.'

'Carol singing as we understand it,' the vicar said, smugly, 'was unknown before the fifteenth century. How do you account for that?'

'They're a progressive crowd,' Dad said. 'They've picked up quite a lot of contemporary stuff since thirteen forty-eight. Jack Pewsey says he heard them having a go at "In the Bleak Midwinter", last year. They don't really mind what they sing, as long as it's got a good tune. The true essence of carol singing, wouldn't you say?' he asked, with a mild smile.

There were no more carols that night. There was no more singing at all, but later, in the early hours of the morning, Emma was woken by a fearful row coming from the street outside. It sounded like tin buckets being kicked downstairs, with a canteen of cutlery by way of descant. She went into her parents' room and found Mum and Dad in dressing-gowns, standing by the window, and looking down into the road.

'I could have told him this would happen,' Dad said, as Emma crept alongside.

'Yes, but I notice you didn't,' said Mum.

'No good flogging a dead horse,' Dad said. 'Still, he may pay attention next year. What on earth have they got down there?'

'Not on earth,' said Mum.

'It sounds like iron kettles and ladles.'

'I suppose it would be.'

'Rough music.'

Emma looked out into the street. In the light of the lamp by the bridge she could see a steady surge of people passing by, silent themselves but raising a deafening clangour from the pots and pans, tongs, hammers and billhooks that they carried.

'I think you'd better have another word with our Mr Jarvis in the morning,' Mum yelled, above the racket.

'Do you think it'll be necessary? After all, they've made their point. They've been carol singing for six hundred years, now. They're not going to stop because some hot-rod vicar tries to run Christmas like the Normandy landings.'

'And warn him about Midsummer's Eve.'

'Midsummer Eve's none of his business,' said Dad, 'or mine. Lord alone knows how long *that's* been going on.'

Emma slipped back to her own room and lay listening to the Waits as they came down from Strang St Thomas to play rough music round the vicarage until dawn broke on St Thomas's Day. Through the clashing of iron on iron she heard voices raised, although she could not make out the tune. Whatever they were singing, however, it was not a Christmas carol.

Efflorescence

I don't suppose the tunnel is there any more. It ran under a stretch of disused railway line and the last time I visited the town, about twenty years ago, there was earth-moving equipment at work in the meadow beyond it, and already a row of houses at the end of the footpath. Probably the footpath is a street by now, and no street would have fitted into that tunnel; it was only six feet across. No, I should guess that the old line has gone and the tunnel with it. This may be just as well.

Dennis Willis and I used to walk through the tunnel twice a day, five days a week, on our way to school and back. My school was Coldharbour High; Dennis went to St Augustine's RC. For a long while this didn't matter, but at the beginning of our second year Dennis's twin brothers started at the infant school and Dennis had to escort them there. Dennis thought this was unfair. I thought it was criminally stupid, like asking your pet baa-lamb to take the mastiffs for a walk; not that Raymond and David were actively carni-vorous. They did not hurl themselves at passers-by and gnaw their ankles, they went in more for what is known as structural damage; gate posts, bird baths, windows. Rose bushes and milk bottles were not safe either in their vicinity. In those days the footpath ran alongside a row of cottages with very small unfenced front gardens, where the milk bottles and rose bushes were within easy reach. Dennis had his work cut out.

The upshot of all this was that Dennis had to leave home much earlier than before in order to deliver the twins to the very doorstep of their school because they could not be trusted to walk even the last hundred yards on their own. Once or twice I tried leaving early as well, to give Dennis moral support – and numerical parity, as Dennis would have it – but there were six of us at home, all leaving for various schools and jobs, and in the end I gave up because I was the youngest and always got trampled in the rush for the bathroom. All the others had not only to wash but to shave, except for my mother, of course. I saw less of Dennis on the way home, too. St Augustine's came out fifteen minutes before we did. In the good old days, B T (Before Twins), Dennis used to wait for me by the allotments, where the town end of the tunnel began, but now the extra fifteen minutes were taken up with collecting Raymond and David and somehow we usually managed to miss each other.

I'm not implying that I used to hide, mind you, and we still met in the evenings when it was fine or we didn't have too much homework. Arranging these meetings was a problem as neither of us had a phone, until Dennis discovered the loose brick. It was probably one of the twins who discovered it or more likely loosened it himself. Given time, no doubt, they would have demolished the entire tunnel, but this particular brick was on the edge, at the allotments end, and could be lifted right out. Dennis's idea was that if one of us wanted to communicate with the other he should leave a message on a piece of paper shoved in behind the brick. Each of us would check, as we went through the tunnel, to see if there were anything in the hole.

This worked for about a week until someone else discovered the loose brick. The someone else was Godfrey Rains and he forged a message from Dennis for me to find on the way to school. Then he forged another one from me, which he left for Dennis the same evening. They were identical. 'See you round by the privet bush, back of the pub. 7.30.' Our writing was easy to forge as we, and Godfrey, had attended the same primary school, taught to write, as our parents had been, by ancient Miss Babbington who had herself been taught to write, so rumour had it, by the author of Genesis. When we rendezvoused innocently under the privet bush at the back of the Three Choughs, we were fallen upon by the Rains brothers, Peter Holdstock and Robert Gann. It was clear that we would have to think of something more secret than a loose brick.

This was not so easy, partly because the brick had seemed perfect and once you have enjoyed perfection anything else is bound to feel a bit of a let-down. Also, there really *was* nowhere else that would serve as a hiding place. What we needed was the kind of thing that spies use for a dead letter drop; a telephone box, litter bin, hollow tree, post hole, but there was nothing. Dennis and I lived on opposite sides of the estate; our routes converged only at the footpath which started out running between two chain-link fences and then lay across the meadow past the terraced row of aforementioned cottages with their gardens that had neither fences nor hedges. In case you think that this doesn't sound very cottagey, they weren't thatched country cottages with roses round the door and wall-to-wall hollyhocks; they had been built as railwaymen's dwellings in much the same style as the station only plainer, without any fancy woodwork.

The third problem was that the Rains Gang were now on to us, watching out for what Dennis called clandestine correspondence.

'What we need is a code,' Dennis said. 'Something fantastically complex to mislead the uninitiated.'

'The what?'

'The Rainses,' Dennis said.

'It needn't be *that* complex, then,' I said.

'O K, but it's got to be misleading,' said Dennis. 'It's got to be so misleading that even if they copy it down and show it to someone intelligent, they won't be able to crack it.'

'Oh, that sort of code,' I said. I was in the Scouts at the time, which Dennis was not, and I'd been thinking along the lines of knotted grass stems, bent twigs, circles of stones. I said as much. Dennis's face became pinched with scorn.

'How long do you think that kind of sign would last?' he demanded. 'The Rains Mob would kick it to *fragments*. That's what they're good at. Why do you think Newt Patrol never gets back to base when you're out tracking?'

'I'm in Beaver Patrol,' I said with dignity, for Dennis, I knew, thought little of Scouting for Boys. 'There isn't a Newt Patrol.'

'You exasperate me,' Dennis said. 'Give me a week to cogitate.' I noticed that he didn't imagine that I should be able to come up with something inside a week. Without doubt I did exasperate him. (Dennis is now Brother Dennis of that Cistercian Order commonly known as Trappists, which seems a terrible waste of a huge vocabulary.)

As it happened, it was a week to the day before Dennis and I ran into each other again, in the tunnel, on the way home from school. Dennis was there already, but I guessed that long before I saw him because as I came through the allotments I could see Raymond and David trying to impale each other on the railings that were meant to keep unauthorized persons off the embankment and away from the little black hut on the top of it, alongside the permanent way where, legend had it, a railwayman had once frozen to death during a blizzard in the middle of the last century. Such huts had little brick chimneys and looked enticingly cosy, but knowing what had happened in this one made it seem less cosy.

Raymond and David had no designs on the hut, they were occupied with the railings. There was something uncannily prehensile in the way they went up and down those railings which made me wonder if there wasn't perhaps an orang-utan a couple of generations back in the Willis family, absent-mindedly converted by missionaries. Dennis himself had long arms and rather short legs.

Dennis was under the archway with a stick of chalk, writing something on the brickwork at head height. He didn't hear me approach, owing to his ululating brothers, so I stood behind him and tried to read what he had written.

J TYF BE AE BBO AEIO R SIAOIAEAP-QVBXYZ As I watched he added, AJJOAOIU BST SO I FIAO GGT GOAT

'Goat?' I said. Dennis jumped, spun round and grinned.

'Goat,' he said, 'or toad, or deer, or seal, or –'

'Sheep?' I said.

'Not sheep.'

'Newt?'

'No.'

'Tyrannosaurus rex?'

'No,' said Dennis, 'but boot or suit or bean or soil. *Come down off of that!*' he roared suddenly, as he finally noticed what the twins were up to. 'Look, I'll come round yours this evening and show you – no I won't. I'll meet you.'

'Where?'

Dennis pointed to his row of letters, chalked on the brickwork. 'Where it says; by the phone box.'

'That says, 'I'll meet you by the phone box?'

'It says,' Dennis explained patiently, 'Tonight, 6.30, phone box.'

'All that says Tonight, 6.30, phone box? Isn't there a shorter way?'

Dennis looked hurt. 'This is Rains-proof, at least, I hope it is. Tonight will reveal all.'

'What about the goat?'

'Forget the goat,' Dennis said. 'It could just as easily be a boil.'

The phone box was the only one on the estate, nearer to my house than to Dennis's, and it was very rarely working. But it was a place where everybody met, or hung around on the off-chance of a meeting. It was said of the phone box that if you stood there long enough everyone you knew would go past eventually. This being the case it was also pretty safe. Even the Rains Gang was not foolhardy enough to attempt a frontal attack or even an outflanking manoeuvre, because at least one of my very big brothers was likely to be there, or all three of them.

I set out at 6.25, convinced that either Dennis was on to something good or else was off his trolley. He just looked smug, though, when I spotted him, sitting on the remains of the bench, by the remains of the litter bin, and ignoring the shuffling and snogging that went on all round him. When he saw me he got up and I saw he was carrying an exercise book. I was in for a period of instruction.

'Where shall we go?' I said.

'Back to yours?' he suggested.

'Well, you could have come round mine anyway,' I said, crossly. 'You needn't have hauled me out here.'

'Ah,' said Dennis, 'but I told you, didn't I, we had to see if it was Rains-proof.'

I looked round. There were no Rainses about.

'It could take *them* a week to decipher it if you just wrote it out backwards.'

'Never underestimate your adversary,' Dennis said, darkly, or as you and I might put it: the Rains Gang may not be as thick as we think.

We walked back to my house rapidly, because I was in a hurry to find out how the code worked and Dennis was dying to tell me. Also, I was only too aware that even if the Rainses hadn't cracked it, neither had I. Indoors we sat at the table and Dennis opened his book. There was the tantalizing message again.

JTYFBEAEBBOAEIORSIAOIAEAPQVBXYZA
JJOAOIUBSTSOIFIAOGGTGOAT

'Got it yet?' Dennis asked, after I had studied it for a few minutes.

'Almost,' I lied. Dennis smiled silently and said,

'Here's the misleading bit. This says exactly the same,' and he wrote:

LPTJROEASMIUIUIDPOIIUEOASFXPBNJO
LSAEAOIRNCCEIJOAEMPKBOIL

'Said it could just as easily be a boil,' Dennis murmured.

'That says the same? Tonight, 6.30, phone box?'

'Or,' said Dennis, 'KSVCRO –'

'All right!' I yelled. 'I give in. How's it done?'

'It's done,' said Dennis, 'on bricks.'

'Bricks?'

'Remember where I was writing it?'

'In the tunnel.'

'On the bricks,' Dennis said. 'It only works on the bricks. That's the misleading part.' I gawped at him. 'Look, when I wrote it in the tunnel it looked like this, didn't it?' He pointed to the first string of letters.

'Almost,' I said again, but this time I meant it. There *was* a difference. 'There were gaps.'

'Like this?' Dennis wrote again:

J TYF BE EA BBO AEIO R SIAOI AEAPQ VBXYZ AJJO AOIU BST SO I FIAO GGT GOAT

'Not quite. Some of those words ran together.'

'They only looked as if they did,' Dennis said. 'I wrote one word on each brick, so of course, the four and five letter words seemed to run together. What you saw in the tunnel was:'

J TYF BE AE BBO AEIO R SIAOIAEAPQVBX-YZAJJOAOIU BST SO I FIAO GGT GOAT

'This –' he pointed to the previous line, '– is what it really says.' He added, 'You're not going to get it, are you?'

'No,' I admitted, and then I suddenly saw what he

had done. 'Hang on!' I wrote: IOU LBW AAA

'Let's hope it never comes to that,' Dennis said. I think he was slightly sorry that I had worked out the code, but he *had* given me a lot of help. We shook hands, solemnly.

'Give it a few more days,' Dennis said. 'We'll write up another test piece and if the Rainses still don't get it, we'll put it into production.'

What Dennis wrote in the tunnel read, brick for brick; WHO GMT LEA EARO USA I BEST OMO AT EE TO UEO OU AAA IP UFO IN Z which, had Godfrey Rains been able to translate it, would have brought the gang down on us like Attila and the Huns, since it actually said, GODFREY RAINS IS A RAT. I'd been practising at home, so when I passed under the railway arch and saw Dennis's message strung out along a course of brickwork I could read it almost without hesitating, but then, I knew the brick trick. When I came home that evening Godfrey himself and Robert Gann were standing, staring at it.

'This yours?' Godfrey said, moving to block my path.

'Nah.' I joined in the staring. 'WHOGMTLE-AEAROUSAIBESTOMO . . . I best Omo? *Pufoinz?* It's a code, innit?'

Robert was copying it down on the back of his hand, but although I knew it was unlikely to get washed off I could see that there was little chance of his deciphering it before wind and rain faded it away. WHOG-MTLEAEARO . . . he printed, laboriously. Godfrey, meanwhile, tried to erase it in the hope of spoiling somebody's fun, but chalk is harder to wipe from brick than from almost anything else. Dennis's code was definitely Rains-proof.

When, after a week, we still hadn't been beaten to pulp, we put the code into operation. It wasn't merely Rains-proof, it was everybody-proof, that infuriating combination of real words, initials, acronyms and meaningless groups of letters. Sometimes a frustrated would-be cryptographer vented his spleen by interfering with our messages, but we could always spot an altered letter, and imitations were nonsense – up until just before half-term, that is. I remember the date exactly.

To foil imitators we had taken to ending messages with the date, and it was always the first thing I checked. As the days shortened it was so dim in the tunnel by home-time that I now carried a torch, and I had to look carefully for today's message, for by now the tunnel looked as if someone had sprayed it with alphabet soup; we had begun to write over our old white messages in red or blue chalk. I stood in the hollow darkness skimming the walls for the signal, which would be that day's date. I couldn't find it and I was just coming to the conclusion that Dennis had written nothing that day when I noticed, far up in the arch of the tunnel, a row of marks, higher than any of us could reach. I read them with ease.

LLLII LII IL LILL III

Now, according to our code, that did actually say something, and my first reaction was fury that at last someone had cracked it. Then I began to wonder; we had never done it using only two letters although that, as this proved, was perfectly possible, and the ones used here are about the simplest letters there are. Not even a baby would have had much trouble with I and L; not even a Rains. I also wondered who on earth would go to all the trouble of climbing up to write on the very top of the arch – climbing up on what? Shoulders? The arch was about ten feet high. I had a vision of the Rains Gang, lightweight Godfrey perched on taller Robert or fat brother Desmond, falteringly tracing those simple letters in haste before his scaffolding collapsed. I felt betrayed – and nervous.

There was no need to write down the message; once I knew what it said I could easily re-encode it, and next morning I went round to Dennis's house and wrote it out for him.

'Someone's on to us, Den,' I said.

Dennis, refusing to panic, looked at what I had written. He said, 'On the roof of the arch, you say?'

'Right at the top of the curve.'

'Depends which way up you look at it from,' Dennis said. He turned the paper round. 'It could say, One thousand, one hundred and seventeen billion . . .' he was good at maths, too, 'seven hundred and seventeen million . . .'

'Come off it, Willis,' I snapped. 'That says eight days. You know it does.'

'Funny sort of message,' Dennis said. 'Eight days of what?'

'Eight days *to* what?'

'To the end of the month?'

'Hallowe'en,' I said.

Dennis counted. 'Thirty days hath September, April, June . . . You're right.' He looked at me uncomfortably. 'Someone's mucking about.'

'Yes, and they're mucking about with our code.'

'Let's go and look,' said Dennis.

It was dark in the tunnel even in summer. Now,

halfway through a dull autumn morning, it was gloomy, but we had the torch. I flashed it up into the tunnel's vault. The letters had faded a little, it seemed to me, since yesterday afternoon, but I hardly noticed that. Below them, on the next course but one, was a second set.

LLIII LII IL LILL III

'That doesn't say one trillion anything,' I said.

'Seven days,' Dennis muttered. He read the letters aloud, 'Lliiiliiillillliii,' a nasty gibbering whine.

'Shut up,' I said, not liking it at all. 'Someone *is* mucking about.'

'That's not chalk,' Dennis said. 'It's not written in chalk.'

'You can't tell from here.'

'Bend down,' said Dennis.

'What for?'

'So I can stand on your shoulders.'

'You're a stone heavier than I am,' I said. 'You bend down.'

Dennis crouched. I climbed on to his shoulders and balanced myself against the wall as Dennis slowly straightened up. Idiotic words slid past my eyes as I rose: GGA . . . OSP . . . GRAW . . . OOOI . . . MARB . . . ULP . . . Dennis turned gingerly and I braced my hands against the curve of the roof.

'Can you see anything?' Dennis said.

I reached out cautiously and touched today's letters, LLIII . . . 'It's not chalk.' The marks were white, but a blue-white, like crystals, and when I touched them a faint crust crumbled under my finger, leaving the marks on the bricks. 'It's more like salt.'

'Efflorescence,' Dennis said, predictably. He teetered and I fell off.

'Fluorescence?'

'Efflorescence. Salts coming to the surface in brick-work – well, not just in brickwork; stones, breezeblocks, even.'

'You mean it's just chance, those marks?' I'd skinned my knee.

'Damn funny chance,' Dennis growled, wiping my boot prints from his shoulders. We stood looking up at the letters.

'Could be coincidence,' I said. Dennis glared, I was pinching one of his long words. Dennis was definitely Holmes. I was only Watson.

'Coincidence, my foot,' said Dennis. 'Those marks weren't put *on* the brick – they came out of it.'

'You mean, we called them out?'

We were both staring at those lines and lines of letters.

'One thousand, one hundred and seventeen billion billion, seven hundred and seventeen billion, seven hundred and eleven million, one hundred and seventy-one thousand, one hundred and seventeen,' Dennis droned.

The next day was Sunday but I went down to the tunnel, just to check. There was a third line of letters: LIIII LII IL LILL III

Six days.

Each line was lower than the last. By the time it had reached IILLL LII IL LILL III, two days, whatever *it* was, the words were about seven feet from the ground. You could see that in two days' time they would be at shoulder level – an adult's shoulder, that is. On the morning of the thirty-first, which was a Saturday,

Dennis and I met by prior arrangement (the usual prior arrangement; we refused to be scared off) and went along to the tunnel to see what was there. The inscriptions of the last week seemed to glow faintly above us in the vault, from the almost illegible LLLII LII IL LILL III down to yesterday's, still sharp and clear: ILLLL LII IL LILL; one day.

We looked everywhere, but there was nothing else written that hadn't been put there by us or our envious imitators, in chalk. We decided not to go through the tunnel again until Monday.

That night Mum, Dad and my three brothers went to

a Hallowe'en party on the other side of town, a grown-up affair with drink; nothing in it for me. I could have gone with them but Dennis's mum said I might stay at theirs, and the two of us sat up half the night cogitating (Dennis, of course) on what might be happening in the tunnel. We were almost tempted to go out and look, and were almost glad that Dennis's mother forbade us going anywhere.

When I went home next morning the house was in an uproar. It had been a very cold night all over the region but in our house the temperature must have hit fifteen below. The garden was white with rime and every chrysanthemum, dahlia and late-flowering rose was blighted and black. The windows were thick with frost ferns and indoors the pipes had frozen. People rushed about murmuring of freak weather conditions and fires were lit, whereupon the pipes, which had burst, thawed dramatically. Plumbers were called. Gradually the house warmed up, but not before I had been into my bedroom. I have never known such cold; it took the breath away, that, and the curious marks in the ice on the window: L LLL LI II LLI IIII L

Tonight.

Neither of us ever went through the tunnel again. If it is still there I doubt if I would go through it even now. Even twenty years on it would seem like putting my luck at risk, and there were several elements of luck in the whole affair. I consider that I had a very lucky escape, although it was several weeks before I had another good night's sleep. It was luck, too, that our correspondent didn't go to Dennis's house, which he might well have done, considering it was Dennis's code that fetched him. Dennis didn't say much when I told him what had happened, but I can't help wondering if that didn't have something to do with his abandoning the idea of becoming a cryptographer and entering a monastery instead. I never spoke of it to anyone else although, much later, I asked my dad in a casual way if he knew anything about the railwayman who was alleged to have died in that little black shack beside the permanent way, just beyond the tunnel.

'He was a telegraphist,' said Dad. 'You know, dot-dot-dot-dash,' and he tapped on the table with bunched fingers, operating an imaginary buzzer. So it was sheer *bad* luck, obviously, that there should be someone using the tunnel who was not misled by Dennis's version of the Morse Code.

NOTHING TO BE AFRAID OF

The characters in Jan Mark's stories are the sort of people who create their own imaginary world of horrors – and then get trapped in it because these are the sort of horrors that won't go away. They follow you upstairs in the dark and slide under the bed, and there they stay . . . Meet young William who has his own version of a well-known tale, irritating Arthur who thinks he knows everything, poor Brenda who's caught between the animosity of two teachers, and a host of other strange and cunning characters.

THUNDER AND LIGHTNINGS

Victor was the oddest boy Andrew had ever met. How could he be so dim in school, and yet know so much about aeroplanes? But as their friendship grew, Andrew became more and more concerned about what would happen when Victor discovered that the Lightnings he loved so much were all to be scrapped. Winner of the Penguin/Guardian competition and the Carnegie Medal for 1976, this was Jan Mark's first book.

TROUBLE HALF-WAY

Amy knew her worrying sometimes drove Richard mad, but she did have plenty to worry about. Grandad was in hospital so Mum had gone with baby Helen to look after Grandma and left Amy with a new stepfather she still felt awkward with. Worse still, Richard wanted to take her Up North delivering furniture in his lorry. Of course, it might be fun doing something so unfamiliar, but Amy wasn't going to start enjoying it without doing her fair share of worrying first.

UNDER THE AUTUMN GARDEN

They were studying local history at school, and since Matthew was head boy, he felt he ought to do a really good project. He knew that his garden lay over the remains of an old priory, so why not dig it up and see what exciting relics he could discover? But Matthew's plan turns sour as all kinds of people interfere. He would never have started if he'd known the obstacles before him.

RT, MARGARET AND THE RATS OF NIMH
Jane Leslie Conly

When Margaret and her brother RT get lost in the forests surrounding Thorn Valley, help comes from an unexpected quarter when the super-rats of NIMH come to their rescue. Margaret and RT must return home before winter sets in, but the incredible events of their summer in the valley become the biggest secret they have ever had to keep.

The third thrilling story in this classic trilogy about the rats of NIMH.

ONLY MIRANDA
Tessa Krailing

A new town, a tiny flat over the Chinese takeaway, a new school mid-term and a place next to Chrissie Simpson, the most unpopular girl in the class. Things aren't looking great for Miranda. But her father has gone to prison and this at least is a chance of a new life for her and her mother. Miranda bounces back in true style: she befriends poor Chrissie and when the dinner money is stolen and Chrissie is suspected, Miranda is determined to prove her innocence.

TWIN AND SUPER TWIN
Gillian Cross

Ben, David and Mitch had only meant to start the Wellington Street Gang's bonfire, not blow up all their fireworks as well. But even worse is what happens to David's arm in the process. Until, that is, they realize that this extraordinary event could be very useful in their battles with the Wellington Street Gang.

HANDS UP! AT JUG VALLEY JUNIORS
Anne Digby

Ben couldn't guess the trouble he would cause when he accidentally kicks Charlie Smith's old football into the rector's garden. When Ben and his friends in Handles & Spouts search the garden after school, there's no sign of the ball. They get Charlie a new one, but Charlie is desperate to find the old ball. Who can have taken it, and why does Charlie want it back so badly? Handles & Spouts have some surprises in store in this third story of a fantastic new series.

THE PHOTOFIT MYSTERY AT JUG ALLEY JUNIORS
Anne Digby

Esme asks the members of Handles & Spouts to watch the house she and her father used to live in. It's supposed to be empty since her father moved to New Zealand to get a better job, and she moved in with her aunt. Missing her father terribly, Esme has noticed little things which have been moved, as though someone is still living in the old house.

Handles & Spouts decide to piece together a photo-fit description to identify the mysterious person in the fourth brilliant adventure of this exciting series.

MISSING
James Duffy

One evening, Kate Prescott is approached by a man in a large black car. He seems friendly and says he knows her mother, so Kate accepts a lift from him. It doesn't take Kate long, however, to realize the dreadful mistake she has made. But will the chief of police be convinced that she really is in danger when she's reported missing?